A Storm on the Horizon

The Xander Bane Chronicles: Book Two

By
Joshua Griffith

ISBN: 9781735078434

Contact Joshua Griffith on Facebook

Follow him on Twitter

Or on his webpage

Cover Art by Getcovers

To all my readers, thank you for your support

Table of Contents

Chapter One

"It's done," Selandra exclaimed as she slipped the dagger into her belt.

"Great, now portal us elsewhere. I'll keep them off you the best that I can."

The Peacekeeper nodded as she pulled out her staff and worked on the portal. The Dampire raced around the roof at inhuman speed, slashing and hacking at anything that moved. He growled angrily as his eyes went full crimson, his hunger demanding blood. As the portal coalesced, Selandra called out, "Time to go, Xander."

The Dampire teleported himself onto the mage's back as she moved through the portal. Xander dropped to the ground as they reappeared with his sword ready. Several reanimated corpses managed to get through the portal before it collapsed.

"Give me the dagger," Xander stated with his hand out.

The mage dropped it into his tiny hand. He slipped it into his belt and walked over to the reanimated corpses, allowing them to grab hold of him.

"What are you doing?" Selandra exclaimed as he was forcefully yanked off the ground.

Xander grinned at the mage and said. "Be right back, Sel."

The Dampire teleported away with the undead creatures, causing Selandra to reach out instinctively for him. She worried that whatever plan he had might go amiss, despite his cunning intellect and speed. The Peacekeeper wasn't sure what would happen if someone was to be bitten by the undead and frankly, she didn't want to think about it.

Xander appeared at the entrance of the enclave where the Mother Vile once thrived. He teleported from the reanimated corpses grasp and reappeared on top of the stone-cold cauldron.

"Come on, you two can do better than that," he taunted as he lifted the lid up and slung it like a disc. The impact tore a leg off each corpse, causing them to collapse. Despite this, the corpses kept moving forward. Xander was mildly impressed with their tenacious desire to feed on him.

He walked over and unsheathed his energy sword. It ignited brightly as the Dampire hacked away at the decaying fiends. He picked up the body parts and tossed them in the putrid humanary stew, humming a little tune to himself. The Dampire snatched up the heads, both still trying to bite him, and plopped them in the cauldron, along with the enchanted dagger.

Xander put the lid back in place and used his weapon to seal it shut. He grinned as he ignited the fire beneath the cauldron.

"Soup's ready," Xander announced as he saw more of the undead appearing from the tree line. He teleported himself onto the top of the largest of the trees and observed the reanimated horde stalking the cauldron. They banged and clawed at the cast iron, but couldn't find a way to open it. The smell of burning decaying flesh wafted in the air, causing Xander to cover his nose.

He turned around and observed how the dead were coming to this place. The Dampire noticed a small tear in the woods, hovering off the ground. It shimmered as light reflected off it. As more reanimated corpses stepped through it, the gap widened, enabling Xander to see beyond the tear.

The architecture of the room was definitely from the Crimson Pass, he'd recognize the stonework anywhere. He saw what appeared to be a mage of some kind, waving a dagger in his hand dramatically as he conjured his magic.

The Dampire decided that it would be prudent to pay a visit to this person. After all, he was the one sending hordes of dead people after him and Sel. He teleported himself onto the caster's back, shocking him. As Xander teleported them to where Selandra was at, he hissed, "You want me? Well, you got me. Let's go have a little fun together, Dampire style!"

Having drank from the Peacekeeper, Xander only needed to think of her and instantly teleport to her. The caster yelped as Xander bit down into his neck, causing him to drop his staff. Selandra saw the man's face and instantly recognized him.

"Where did you find Merrick and why are you drinking from him?"

"He chose to donate to the cause, so naturally, I accepted. Though his blood tastes peculiar."

Selandra walked over as the Dampire released the conjurer, taking Merrick's dagger with him. She lifted his head up roughly by his curly blonde hair, unable to believe her eyes. "I heard word that you perished during your raid on the ogre encampment three years ago."

Merrick smiled, half loopy from the blood loss. "Obviously, you heard correctly. As you can see, I'm alive and thriving now. Join me."

Chapter Two

Confused, the Peacekeeper asked, "Join you? What are you slurring on about?"

Xander sat down on a nearby stump, cleaning his claws with Merrick's dagger as he answered, "Summoning dead people, of course."

"What?" Selandra looked over at the Dampire, trying to assess if he was joking. He met her gaze and stated, "Just ask him. Merrick here is into necromancy."

"I can do what the Great Wizard couldn't do. In death, I've mastered death!" Merrick growled at the Dampire.

"Sounds like a dead-end career, if you ask me." The Dampire grinned.

"You know nothing, *abomination*!" Merrick spat as Selandra bound his hands behind his back with a small piece of rope. "This is who I am now."

"But why didn't you return to the spire? Why let us believe that you died?"

"I died and now, I live. There's nothing at the spire for me. I'm above it and its archaic teachings. I'm free to do whatever I want and I get handsomely paid for my skills."

"So, you're in the employ of the council?" Xander asked as he surveyed his surroundings. They were within a small grove of apple trees, though from the looks of it, not many have traveled through it in some time. Far to the left was the remnants of a wagon cart road, where the tall grass had nearly consumed it.

The wildlife seemed to be flourishing here as different song birds chirped and a small herd of deer fed on the fallen fruit on the ground. A stream could be heard not far in the distance, Xander's acute hearing detected something splashing about in the water. He wondered what the significance of this place had to Selandra.

"I don't have to dignify that with an answer, especially to you, *abomination!*" the conjurer hissed.

"Ah, either my reputation precedes me or you just answered my question." The Dampire grinned as he tossed the dagger around the air.

Merrick incredulously gasped as he watched the Dampire. "Stop doing that, it's not a toy to play with! It's a powerful weapon and-"

"It will destroy us all if not properly trained in using it?" Selandra interrupted, hoping that she guessed wrong. Xander didn't seem to care at all as he stabbed the blade in the ground and into the stump he sat on.

"I'm not going to say." Merrick sneered at the Peacekeeper, then looked back at the Dampire. "He will end up killing himself, so my task will be complete."

"I highly doubt it," Xander responded as he walked over and held the tip of the dagger by Merrick's eye. "I'm fairly certain that it needs blood to activate it. I can smell your blood on it. My question is: Does it still have enough blood on it to be dangerous? Here, you look at it and tell me if it does."

The Dampire jabbed the dagger into the conjurer's eye, causing him to scream and thrash. Selandra pulled Merrick up to his knees, glaring at the Dampire. "Why did you do that?"

"I want to see if he can still use it. How about it, Merrick? Can you summon with it or not?"

He spat on the Dampire as blood trickled down his face, groaning in pain. "Hand it here and let me show you, *abomination*!"

Xander walked over and wiped the spit off him and on the conjurer's hair as he stabbed the blade into both of his hands. Merrick cried out, pleading with the Peacekeeper. "Get this freak under control!"

She watched as Xander methodically twisted the knife, he leaned in and coldly asked, "If you refuse to answer me, then consider talking with your old friend there. She asks, you answer. You refuse, I carve on you with your own knife. It's as simple as that, Merrick."

He nodded as he grimaced, waiting for the Peacekeeper to question him. She watched the Dampire slowly walk in a circle around them. He licked the blade as he came into Merrick's view, still puzzled by the taste.

"Why are you doing this? What purpose does necromancy serve?"

"Power. Power to create a race of soldiers that doesn't need sleep, nor rest, or comforts. They obey without question. Have you ever wondered what it would be like to command such a team? You would be unstoppable."

"And yet, you were stopped," Xander pointed out.

"Dumb luck on your part, Dampire." Merrick fumed as he turned his head to see Selandra. "Join me and I will teach you how to unlock this power, as well as other skills."

"You're asking me to forsake the spire, the Great Wizard Zerron, and the Peacekeeper's oaths?"

Merrick grinned. "You could be greater than all the Peacekeepers, including Zerron."

"A wonderful offer," Xander snapped his fingers, "where do I sign up?"

"You're not welcome, *abomination*! This offer is solely for the best mage I know. Selandra, I've trained with you. I know your ambitions, how you want to bring the killer of your family squirming into the burning light."

"I wanted that, once." Selandra honestly answered. "But things change. I've grown since having those fantasies. The culprits have probably already been staked."

Merrick smirked, "I have a source that says otherwise. She knows exactly who did it."

"And this source is?" Selandra impatiently asked.

"Your mother."

Selandra fumed, barely able to control her outrage. "What. Are. You. Saying?"

Merrick smugly grinned. "Long ago, I tracked down the burial site of your parents. I wanted to give you the ultimate gift: the name of the vampire that destroyed your family."

Selandra slowly sat down on the stump, dumbfounded by the conjurer's claim. She glared at him as she hissed, "You violated her burial site and raised her from the dead, just to ask who killed her? Why?"

"I've admired you from afar for years. I knew that if I could give you the name of the monster that slaughtered your parents, you would be grateful and we could go off and hunt him down."

"And then you two could live happily ever after." Xander grinned. Selandra scowled at him as he made kissing noises and moaned Merrick's name in a feminine voice.

The mage returned her attention to their prisoner and stated, "You actually thought that was the way to win my heart and affection: raise my dead mother from the grave, us going on an epic adventure, and somehow I'd have to look past your desecration of the only family that I knew and fall madly in love with you?"

Merrick gave a wry smile. "When you put it that way, it does sound a bit-"

"Pathetic?" the Dampire piped up.

"Sad," the Peacekeeper said in disgust. "You'll be coming back to the spire with us and answer to the Great Wizard."

"You won't be taking me back to that old poser of the spire," Merrick announced as he managed to stand up. A spark of light flashed from behind his back as he freed himself. The conjurer balled up his fist, his magic pulsated brightly.

Chapter Three

Merrick grinned maniacally as he cast magical energy at the Dampire from his now healed hands. Xander was struck as the magic slammed into his chest. Selandra unsheathed her sword as she let bursts of magic fly from the tip of her staff.

Merrick managed to block all the Peacekeeper's attacks, much to Selandra's astonishment.

"My fight isn't with you, Selandra!"

"You fight Xander, then you fight me." She countered as she slashed her sword at Merrick.

He evaded each strike as he called his dagger to his hand, "This is unfortunate. You throw your lot in with *that,* and not me? I plan on taking his head off and giving it to you as a trophy."

"Why the hell would I want my partner's head as a trophy? You've gone mad."

Xander teleported himself onto Merrick's back, but before the Dampire could bite him, the conjurer let loose a full body blast of energy. It knocked Xander about ten feet away and Selandra down to the ground. Merrick growled at the fallen Dampire, "Not this time, *abomination!*"

He charged after Xander, looking to make good on his promise. Merrick stopped and stabbed his blade into the ground, muttering an incantation.

"Careful," Xander mocked as he rubbed the back of his head, "you might break your little toy doing that."

Merrick smirked as he finished his incantation, the ground around the two of them shook. The Dampire cried out in agony as multiple roots exploded from the ground underneath him, each one burrowing through his diminutive body.

All of his limbs had at least three roots impaling them, his torso had twice as many. Another root wrapped around Xander's forehead, pinning his head back and exposing his neck.

Merrick slowly stood up and arrogantly stood over to the Dampire. He triumphantly towered over Xander and mocked, "At least I know what I can do with my dagger. It's great for protection and casting spells, but my favorite use will be taking your head off!"

"Hurry up," Xander growled defiantly through the pain, "decapitate me before your monologuing ends me first."

The conjurer kneeled down by him with the blade to Xander's neck. "Tell me, *abomination*, how many times have you tried to teleport away from this?"

"Why should I..." Xander coughed up blood, "when I have you...right where I want you..."

Selandra shook her head as she watched in horror as Merrick dug the dagger's edge into Xander's throat, like he was cutting into a slab of meat. She grasped her staff with both hands and with as much will as she could put behind it, she unleashed a blast of magic at the conjurer.

Merrick pulled his dagger up just in time to not only block the attack, but deflect it at Xander.

"NO!" Selandra screamed as she heard the gurgling cry of anguish that escaped from Xander's mouth.

"Your aim is off, Selandra," Merrick mocked as he pointed his dagger at the helpless Dampire. "This is the direction it should've gone. Don't worry, I corrected that misfire." He stabbed Xander multiple times and added, "This is who you should be attacking, not me."

Selandra picked up her sword and charged at Merrick once more. "I said leave my partner alone!"

Merrick smirked as he stabbed Xander again and muttered, "She was always a little too feisty and headstrong. I see nothing has changed."

He stood up and held his dagger with both hands. Selandra thrusted her sword, aiming for Merrick's heart, but her blade was repelled. She hacked and slashed but couldn't get through the conjurer's protection.

"Such passion. Such conviction. You would be a powerful ally in the upcoming war. Join me, Selandra, and I can teach you techniques like this one and so many more."

"Never!" the Peacekeeper hissed. Her anger intensified when she saw Xander's prone body, his blood saturating the ground. "Unlike you, I take my oaths as a Peacekeeper seriously!"

Xander eyed the one-sided fight. He wasn't sure if listening to the conjurer was making his head hurt or possibly the massive amount of blood loss. Consciousness was becoming more of the struggle, one that he was losing.

The arrogance of Merrick irked the Dampire that he wanted nothing more than to smash his better-than-thou grin off his face. He smiled as he thought of the perfect way to do it.

Selandra's strength waned as her attacks lessened. Merrick smirked as he spoke again. "You see, I've not had to do any kind of exertion like you and because of that, I could easily kill you where you stand. I might as well, since you refuse to join me. I can always raise you from the dead and then we could fight together once more. Maybe I can bed you before the rotting takes over."

Before the Peacekeeper could reply, Merrick sent a barrage of magical beams at her from the dagger. The energy was about the width of an arrow, but to Selandra, they felt like the punches from a prize fighter. Her body bucked and jerked with each strike, until one hit her chin.

She toppled over, lying on her stomach, moaning as Merrick sat down and straddled her back. He yanked her head up by her crimson hair roughly and gleefully hissed, "Why wait until you're dead when I can take you now. I've always wanted you and now I can-ARRGH!"

The conjurer howled in pain as a quick beam of energy cut off his dagger welding hand. Shocked and confused, Merrick rolled off Selandra, ripping a small tuft of hair out in the process. He grabbed his hand and dagger just in time to see an energy blade coming straight for him. He managed to dodge it, but the weapon harassed him no matter what he did.

Merrick stabbed the air, creating a small rift and cried, "This isn't over, Selandra! We will meet again!"

He jumped through just as the energy blade struck his left thigh, causing him to yelp. The rift closed up as Selandra attempted to get up, but her body was racked with pain. The hilt dropped harmlessly to the ground next to the Peacekeeper.

Chapter Four

She picked up Xander's weapon as she crawled over to the Dampire, grimacing in pain. She sat up with her legs bent underneath her and gasped at the damage Xander had sustained. Selandra covered her mouth, stifling a cry, as she reached out and touched one of the roots that was holding Xander helplessly in place.

The root felt wrong and corrupted in many ways, she could feel it draining not only his magic but his life force. Selandra felt light-headed and noticed that she was getting weaker. She tried to pull her hand away from the root, but it resisted coming free.

The Peacekeeper desperately grabbed her forearm and with all her might, she yanked it as she threw her body backwards. Selandra yelped as her hand came free, she clutched it to her chest as she rested on her back.

Panting, Selandra examined her hand and saw that some of her skin had been ripped off and it was throbbing. She stood up gingerly, trying to figure out how to get her partner out of his bindings. Her heart was breaking, seeing the diminutive Dampire in his current state.

Xander's eyes fluttered open, barely focusing on the Peacekeeper. She caressed his forehead, noting that he appeared paler than a regular vampire. He tried to talk but nothing came out, the neck incision prevented anything but raspy noises.

"Oh Xander," Selandra sadly gushed, "I'll try what I can to free you, but I fear that I may kill you in the process. The roots are literally eating your life and magic. I don't-"

Xander's energy blade ignited, causing the mage to pause. She picked it up and was astonished that it remained active for her. This contradicted everything that she knew about this type of weaponry. Energy weapons were wielder specific, no one else could use them, except the rightful owner.

Selandra wondered if the Dampire was controlling it for her. If so, she may not have much time to use it. She touched the energy blade against one of the roots, the one restraining his head. It recoiled and receded back in the ground.

Selandra swiped the blade at the rest of the roots, but before she could get it past his belly, it shut off. She glanced down and saw that the Dampire was unconscious. The Peacekeeper figured that it took a lot of effort and concentration to manage what he did with his weapon.

At least he managed to help free some of his body, the mage mused. Selandra didn't want to jostle him too much, but she needed him awake and alert if she was going to free him.

She held her wounded hand over Xander's gaping mouth and painfully dug her nails into her palm. Blood dripped slowly into the Dampire's mouth. Selandra hoped that it would be what he needed to revive and aid her with his extraction from the roots.

"Xander, wake up!" she pleaded, grimacing as she dug her nails painfully deeper. "Don't you dare leave me. I need you to wake up and help me free you."

Xander's eyes fluttered open once again, much to the Peacekeeper's delight. She put her bloody palm against his lips as she held his weapon.

"Turn it on again and I will get us out of here. Do you understand?"

The blade ignited, but it seemed unstable, winking in and out, which told the mage that she needed to act quickly. She swung it, burning away the roots that the blade touched. Then the blade grew brightly and a blast of energy pulsed over the Dampire's entire body. Selandra could feel the raw power coursing from the hilt, the energy penetrating the ground all around the Dampire.

The blade switched off as Xander went unconscious once again. Selandra leaned down and gingerly picked up his limp body, just in case the roots managed to come back. Selandra walked over and propped the Dampire against the stump, she could see that his breathing was shallow. She walked over to where her sword and staff laid and grabbed them.

The mage grimaced as she sheathed her sword, blood still oozed from her shaky hand. She walked back over to Xander with her staff in hand and stated, "Hold on, partner. I'll get us both home."

She grabbed him by his bloody clothes and managed to drape his limp body over her shoulder. Selandra muttered an incantation and slowly a portal coalesced before her. The mage hobbled through it, sweating under the burden of Xander's weight.

Selandra stepped out by the lake on the outskirts of Le'orn and collapsed on the ground. She panted heavily as she held Xander's body protectively against her. Selandra could see that his wounds were healing but not as fast as they normally would, which meant one thing: Xander needed more blood.

The Peacekeeper wanted to place his lips against her soft neck, but thought better of it, fearing that in his current state that the Dampire would drink her dry. She decided to use her forearm, the one that he viciously tore into when she brought him before the Great Wizard.

Selandra unsheathed her sword. She groaned as she ran the tip deep into her flesh, causing the blood to flow. She forced Xander's mouth open and placed her bloody appendage into his gaping maw and stated, "Drink, Xander. Use me to sustain and heal your wounds."

The Dampire barely opened his teardrop shaped eyes, the Peacekeeper could see that they were completely crimson.

"Please don't drain me, but do drink. I don't want to lose you."

Xander blinked slowly as he used what little strength he had left to hold onto Selandra's arm. She expected to feel his fangs tear into her wound, but he used his tongue to lap at it. The mage watched him intently, still waiting for the pain, but then he heard him speak.

"Don't fret, Sel. I'm going to drink you slowly. I won't hurt you so stop being afraid."

Selandra looked at the Dampire, her eyes widened. "Did you just speak to me telepathically? I didn't know that you could do that!"

Xander shrugged as he mentally spoke again. *"Nor I, but I wanted to try. I wasn't sure if you would hear me. This isn't normal for me."*

"Do you think it has something to do with what Zerron did to you?"

"I wouldn't put it past him being the one responsible for this new skill. Might be why I can hear his voice when he was berating everyone. As much as my body demands that I use my fangs on you, I'm resisting...for your safety."

Selandra's lips parted, then she heard him add, *"I don't want to hurt this part of your body again, Sel. Hmm, I wonder..."*

"What?"

"Talk to me, like this."

"You want to know if it goes both ways?"

Xander nodded. The mage wasn't sure what to say exactly or how to connect with the

Dampire mentally. Yet he made it seem effortlessly easy.

"Xander, can you hear me?"

"Weird, isn't it, Sel?"

Selandra slowly nodded, smiling down at the Dampire. She examined his wounds and saw that most of them were closed with fresh pink skin. The slash on his neck was slowly sealing up. The mage wondered if there would be a scar or if it would appear as though no trauma had happened.

"I'll be my pretty, good looking imp self before you know it, Sel," Xander said as he wiggled his eyebrows at her.

"Great. Now I have to guard my thoughts around you, don't I?"

"I'm answering what I heard. I guess that's something we both should work on together. This will come in handy if we need to secretly scheme amongst our enemies."

"I agree. I wasn't thinking that your scars would make you repulsive. I just wish that we could've killed Merrick."

"His days are numbered, Sel." Xander reached out and caressed her cheek, *"He may have fled, but I've fed on him and I can find him no matter where he hides."*

"Is that the reason you scratched me when I captured you?"

"Yes. Remember, I made the promise to kill you. It's how I would've tracked you down had things turned out differently between us."

Xander pulled his lips from the mage's forearm and rolled on top of her. He cupped her face and gently kissed her soft lips. As he moved his lips along her cheek, Selandra turned her head, exposing her neck to him.

"Do you wish for me to take more?" Xander asked, his voice came out raspy.

"You need to feed. You lost a lot of blood today. Just make sure to take us back to our bed when you're done with me."

"I will because we both could use some much-needed rest and time to figure out what needs to be done about this necromancer."

Selandra nodded and added, "You're going to need some new clothes. I'm not sure that our seamstresses can properly mend your attire."

"This is true," the Dampire replied as he slowly licked the mage's neck several times, causing her to shiver, "but for now, I'm going to drink from my favorite mage."

Chapter Five

A slight pop caused her to gasp, "Oh Xander!"

The Peacekeeper grabbed hold of the Dampire, not wanting to let him go. She felt a small hand snake its way into her pants, his nimble fingers caressing her core. Selandra moaned as her mouth opened, her breathing came in quickly.

"Oh Gods," she moaned as her eyes fluttered, panting and having difficulty speaking, "What if someone...sees us... like this..."

"Then we will give them one hell of a show, Sel," Xander purred next to her ear before slipping his fangs back into her soft skin. She felt the Dampire having some difficulty tugging down her pants so she relinquished her hold on him and assisted in pulling them down. A moment later, the mage was rewarded with a rock-hard member sliding inside her slick core.

Selandra slowly moaned as she bucked her hips in rhythm with each of Xander's thrusts. He removed his fangs from her neck and grabbed her head, eyeing her ravenously. "I won't let that prick touch you again. You are mine and mine alone!"

She met his stare and demanded, "If you mean it, then bring me his head back as a trophy, my love!"

The Dampire grinned. "Gladly!"

As Xander increased his speed, a bellowing voice called out with disgust and revulsion, "So, it's true. You *are* a blood whore!"

The pair looked up and saw Serrock standing nearby, sneering at them. Xander grinned, flashing his bloody fangs at the towering mage. "Sorry to disappoint you, but this is our alone time. Leave now and I won't kill you."

"You dare threaten me, imp?" Serrock growled as he pointed his staff at the Dampire.

"I challenge you to make the first move. It will be your last, if you try anything!"

Selandra kept her eyes closed, feeling embarrassed that Serrock found them being intimate by the lake. She felt Xander's hands grab her arms as he taunted, "My that's a rather large staff you have there. If I didn't know any better, I'd say that you're compensating for the tiny, dangling bits between your thighs."

Selandra couldn't restrain a burst of giggles. Serrock growled as he released a blast of magic at the Dampire. "Why you little abomination! I'll see you dead for that disrespectful comment!"

The Peacekeeper felt the Dampire teleport them away to safety. From the change of the ground to the familiar softness of her bed, she knew that he brought them to her room. Selandra smiled as she opened her eyes, lovingly gazing at Xander. "You make friends everywhere you go, don't you?"

"Some mages just don't have a sense of humor around here. Who was he?"

"That's Serrock, the mage that threatened me before we left for Crimson Pass. The one that you stole his clan members from and gifted to the vampires. I'm fairly certain that I need to keep my door on permanent lockdown."

Xander gave her a wry smile. "I'll be sure to tell him where to find his wayward sheep."

"Please don't," Selandra pleaded. "We already have the vampires, Merrick, the necromancer and her undead after us. Let's not add Serrock and his clan to the list."

"Like you said, I do make friends everywhere I go."

He pulled up Selandra's tunic and hissed at the small round bruises. The Dampire grazed his fingertips over each, causing the mage to flinch.

"Merrick will pay for marring your perfect skin," Xander stated as he ran his tongue over her wounds. The Peacekeeper gasped as she ran her fingers through his slick hair.

Much to her dismay, Xander pulled down her tunic and held her close. Before she could protest, the Dampire stated, "It's been a long day. I believe that you and I could use some much-needed sleep. You might want to tend to your hand, Sel. I can imagine how much pain it's causing you."

Selandra nodded as she rolled out of his grasp. She walked over to the wall, peeled off her clothes and placed them in the hole. She assessed Xander with a hand on her hip. "I'm afraid your clothes have seen better days. I'm not sure that they are mendable, let alone functional."

Xander shrugged. "If it wasn't for your gracious leader, I would go home and change into something that less resembles a pauper's finest clothing." He smiled as he added, "You wouldn't happen to have the key to breaking the wardings?"

"That kind of magic," Selandra answered as she walked into the bathroom, but left the door open. She palpated the different spots on her tender muscles, wincing, "is years beyond my talents. One doesn't get handed the mantle of Great Wizard without having some magical prowess."

"Yet Merrick bested us both. Aren't you considered above him in skills?" The Dampire asked as he placed an arm around her lower back.

"I thought so too, but lately I wonder if I'm above any of the mages here."

"Are you not taught those attacks? Or, at least, how to defend against them?"

"Great," Selandra stated flatly, dropping her arm and crossing them at her navel. "It's bad enough that I'm questioning my own talents, but now I have to hear it coming from your lips too?"

"I'm not judging," Xander answered as he caressed her butt cheeks, "just making my own observations. If anything is apparent to me is that we're severely lacking in information. We're barely getting by on these missions by ourselves. Imagine if a team of mages went in, how many would have returned?"

The mage wasn't sure what to say to that. They got through the scrapes together, but did it reflect more on the Dampire's supernatural abilities? Did her being a part of this partnership even matter?

"From what that mage offered, it did sound tempting," Xander mused as he climbed up on the wall. He crinkled his nose in disgust as he disrobed. "You could've had all that power and be unstoppable. What kept you from joining Merrick?"

"You," Selandra replied as she turned to help the Dampire out of his ruined clothes. "He was making the offer while trying to cut your head off! What more could I do, besides protect my partner?"

"He did seem preoccupied with that," the Dampire stated as he unconsciously rubbed his throat. "Let me guess: he proclaimed me as the killer of your parents?"

"He never said a name, but was hell bent on ending our partnership. Are you in pain?" The mage touched one the bright pink circles of skin lightly, half expecting him to flinch.

"Pain is always a part of me. These wounds will heal. I just need rest, as do you, Sel."

"By the way," Selandra turned the Dampire so that he was facing her, "Thanks. Thank you for protecting me from Merrick."

Chapter Six

The Peacekeeper wrapped her arms around his naked form and held him against her. She wasn't sure if she should relay the events that transpired or not so she stated, "You did what you could from your incapacitated state and that was more than enough to send him fleeing like a coward."

From the increase in her heart rate, Xander knew that there was more to the story, but he chose not to press the matter. Whatever it was caused her a lot of emotional turmoil as well. The Dampire could sense it from the way that she held him and through their newly formed connection. Whatever Merrick did to cause Selandra to feel this way, Xander vowed to gut the gutless conjurer.

"I see," Xander replied as coldly as he could. "Sit down and allow me to mend your hand."

The Peacekeeper walked over and sat down on the toilet, still holding Xander like a shield. "I'm not helpless. I can do it myself."

"Never crossed my mind. I want to do this for you since you saved me. It's the least I can do."

"But I-"

"No buts, Sel." Xander's eyes locked with her as he tenderly placed his forehead against hers, pleading, "Let me tend to this so we can both get some rest."

Selandra resisted for a few moments before she relinquished her hold on the Dampire. He walked over and opened a small box attached to the wall by the mirror. He gathered a roll of bandages and some gauze, as well as a small jar that had a thick green substance in it.

The Dampire sat down on her lap and examined her hand. Selandra shivered uncontrollably as he ran his tongue methodically over her palm. He did this several times before saying, "An extra healing ingredient. My saliva will help speed up the healing process."

Xander removed the cork lid and sniffed the aroma that wafted out of the jar and smiled. "This concoction of yours should do nicely on your hand."

"I made it myself for these kinds of injuries- ouch!" Selandra hissed as he generously coated her wound with the green goo. The Dampire pressed several pieces of gauze on top of the sticky substance and then proceeded to wrap it in place with her bandages.

"Xander?"

"Yes, Sel?"

"Thanks. Let's go to bed and worry about wardrobes tomorrow."

Xander nodded as he slid down quietly onto the floor. He walked over to put the medical supplies back in the storage box as the Peacekeeper sauntered by, feeling exhausted. She smiled as she saw her diminutive partner had teleported himself by the bed, pulling back the covers as he invitingly patted it.

The mage laid down and allowed Xander to tuck her in before he teleported himself on the bed beside her. She looked at him, noting that his eyes were crimson, and whispered, "If you need more blood, do take more."

"I'm fine, Sel. You need to rest."

"I can tell that you need more," the mage answered as she brushed her hand on his cheek. "Your eyes are red and after what you went through today, I know that you need more blood."

"I told you that the bloodlust showing in my eyes doesn't always mean that I need blood. I'm not your average vampire. Food and rest can sustain me just fine."

"Yes, I know this, but I also recall you practically bleeding out today." Selandra pulled the Dampire up onto her chest. She guided his head down into the crook of her neck. "As your handler, I say feed so you can regain your strength. But as your lover, I ask that you do it for me. I want you to recover quickly."

Before Xander could reply, the mage firmly added, "No is not an option here. Drink."

The Dampire sighed heavily. He glided his tongue along her soft skin, causing the mage to pant. With a soft pop, his fangs pierced into Selandra's neck once again, causing a small gasp to escape her trembling lips. The Dampire felt her arms release him as she tried to pleasure herself, but his small form blocked her erogenous zones.

Xander snaked his arms out and grabbed her by the wrists. He pinned her arms above her head and coldly whispered in her ear, "No pleasure. I'm here for feeding only. If I'm being forced to drink from you, then I won't allow you any sexual pleasure."

"Xander, please." Selandra squirmed, trying to grind against his rock-hard form.

"No is not an option here, Sel. You make demands on me, then be prepared for the repercussions because I might drink you dry."

Xander roughly bit back down into the mage's neck before she could reply. She could feel the difference in the way he was feeding on her from earlier at the lake and now. At the lake, it was slow and deliberate; now it felt cold and devoid of care. The Peacekeeper tried to buck him off of her body, but the Dampire didn't budge.

As the blood loss increased, Selandra incoherently blurted out, "Men! You're just...as terrible as...Merrick...He wanted...to rape me...You want to... blood rape me...Just kill me..."

Xander stopped drinking and looked at the mage, who was now crying as her eyes rolled around in bitter anguish. The Dampire wondered if he heard her correctly. He got into her face, Selandra's own blood dripped onto her as he hissed, "What do you mean? When did that prick try that with you?"

Selandra sniffled, "What does it matter? Why would you even care? He tried and failed, unlike *you*."

Xander let go of her wrists as he sat back, straddling her with his arms across his bare chest. "You demanded it and I did it. As you told the council so eloquently earlier, magic comes with a price. So does forcing me to do something against my will, especially if it involves blood. It's primal and not something to play games with, Sel. If I were to blood rape you, this would've been much worse on you. I'll show you when we cross paths again with Merrick."

The mage glared at him through bleary eyes, "You're a bastard, Xander Bane!"

"This is true, but the correct terms are abomination and monster. You best get used to it, deary, because your glorious leader stuck you with one." The Dampire leaned down and buried his face in her neck once more. He licked at the puncture wounds as Selandra half-heartedly slapped his head.

The blows didn't deter Xander nor did it bother him. He knew that she was both furious and weakened from his feeding, so why not let her get it out of her system?

Xander rolled off of the Peacekeeper and off the bed. Selandra watched him walk out of her room without looking back at her before she succumbed to the darkness.

Chapter Seven

Xander walked the halls quietly. He felt some guilt about how he treated the mage, which was new for him. He wasn't used to it, but he knew exactly who to blame for it.

Zerron.

"Damn meddling mage," the Dampire muttered.

As he rounded the corner, the Dampire was met by the hulking mage. Serrock sneered in disgust, something Xander was used to experiencing. He attempted to get around the mountain of a man, but the mage blocked him each time.

"It's bad enough that you exist and reside here," Serrock growled as he looked down at the Dampire, "but must you indecently walk these halls?"

"Blame your ancient leader for this, not me," Xander replied matter of fact towards the mage's attitude. "If I had a say, I wouldn't be here with you uptight prudes in the first place.

Now, if you don't mind, I'd much rather be in the company of myself."

Serrock sneered, "Where's your blood whore? She needs to be held accountable for your behavior."

"She's been busy doing her job, so she's resting. Unlike you, we've been out discerning the threat level of the necromancer. The Great Wizard Zerron will want to hear this. Do you know where he's at currently?"

Serrock glowered down at the diminutive Dampire as he crossed his muscular arms across his barrel chest. "He's in his study and mustn't be disturbed by the likes of you, *abomination*."

Xander chuckled. "Like you can stop me."

The mage snarled as reached down and brandished an energy sword at the Dampire. He slashed and stabbed at him, but Xander effortlessly dodged each strike. He cackled while mocking, "Is this the best that you can do? I've heard that you're one of the best mages here. From what I've seen so far, those were nothing more than tall tales."

Serrock fired blasts from his energy sword at the Dampire, the attacks struck everything except his target as Xander teleported, grinning at the mage.

"Stand still, *abomination*!"

"Why?" Xander retorted. "Can you only hit stationary targets? It says a lot about you. Now, let's test your defenses!"

Xander teleported under the mammoth mage. He swiped his claws at the bends of his knees and then he severed both of his Achilles tendons, shredding clean through the mage's thick leather boots. Serrock cried out as he collapsed on the floor.

Xander walked up the downed mage's back, causing him to painfully growl while flailing his arms at the Dampire. "Get off me, vermin! Fight me like a man!"

Xander snatched both of Serrock's arms by his wrists and snapped them both with little effort. The mage screamed as the

Dampire stepped on the floor, picking up the deactivated energy sword. He pointed it at Serrock as he stated, "I'd rather fight you as the abomination that I am and not a pathetic man, such as yourself."

"Trying to figure it out?" Serrock sneered as sweat coated his face. "It only obeys me! You're not worthy of such a great weapon!"

"I know this. I'm just ensuring that if you try to activate it again, you will be on the messy end of it. That said." Xander grasped the hilt with both of his tiny hands and effortlessly broke it with his super strength.

"No!" Serrock cried out, he could only watch as the Dampire crumpled both pieces into wads of metal and let them drop harmlessly on the floor. The Dampire grabbed a handful of the mage's hair and pummeled his face. Xander got in the dazed mage's periphery and coldly stated, "Let's go pay Zerron a visit, shall we?"

He teleported them directly to the outside of the Great Wizard's study. The Dampire knocked on one of the double doors as Serrock emptied the contents of his stomach on the floor.

"Interesting." The Dampire raised an eyebrow. "Selandra has a stronger constitution than you do. At least she can handle teleportation with ease."

The doors to study opened, Zerron was caught off guard by the sight at the threshold. He shook off the initial shock of seeing the battered and broken mage and a skyclad Dampire and asked, "What is the meaning of this intrusion? What happened to Serrock?"

"*I* happened." Xander glared as he dragged the mage into the room by his hair, he sneered and decided to keep his report to himself. "He picked a fight and I was more than happy to oblige."

Zerron walked over and examined the bloody mage. He raised an eyebrow. "Was it necessary to do all that to him, Master Bane?"

"I held my end up of the bargain and didn't kill him." Xander slammed Serrock's face into the floor, breaking the mage's nose.

Serrock groaned in pain as the diminutive Dampire laid down on the mage's back with his hands behind his head, eyeing Zerron with contempt. "I already warned you to keep your mages in check. The next one that falls out of line, like this mountainous moron, I *will* kill them."

"Noted," Zerron said as he sat down at his desk, perusing through various parchments. "How did your mission go at Crimson Pass? Did you glean any information?"

Xander impassively gazed at the leader of the mages. "I'm not here to report, just dropping off the garbage."

Zerron glanced up from the parchments, unamused. "You're in servitude to me so you *will* answer me."

"This is true," the Dampire pointed out as Serrock tried to shake him off his back, "but I'd rather do it with my partner present."

"That's simple enough to rectify."

As the Great Wizard went to summon her with his emerald ring, Xander chimed in. "She's in no state to speak, let alone stand, at the moment. I had to drink much of her blood."

"Get off me, *abomination*!" Serrock roared. "You and your blood whore should be thrown out of the spire! You - Oof!"

The Dampire shifted and gave the mage a quick, downward kick on the back of his head with his heel. Serrock was rendered unconscious as Xander rolled off his limp body and teleported himself onto the top of Zerron's desk. He placed his small arms across his chest with a smirk. "When we both recover, you'll get your information. In the meantime, deal with your broken mountain and have him back off my handler. His threats won't go unpunished. If not by you, then it will be by my hands."

"I will talk with Serrock." Zerron averted his eyes from the skyclad Dampire down to Serrock. He twisted the stone on his ring, calling several mages to come to his study.

"Please remove yourself from my desk. I have much work to do and I don't have time for your antics."

The mages appeared at the study doorway and gasped. Zerron waved at Serrock and ordered, "Take him to the healers."

The mages rushed in and lifted Serrock up by his bulky arms, grunting under the strain of his dead weight. One asked Zerron, "What happened to him, Great Wizard?"

Xander teleported himself onto the giant mage's shoulders and coldly threatened, "*I* happened. Don't ask stupid questions. Leave us be or I will show you what else I can do."

Xander teleported off Serrock and let the mages struggle with the unconscious mage's dead weight as they exited the study. The Great Wizard kept getting distracted by the Dampire's presence and impatiently asked, "What do you want?"

Xander grinned as he motioned to his naked form. "Isn't it obvious?"

"If you soiled your attire, just put them in the laundering box in Selandra's room."

"Does it repair torn fabric?"

Zerron raised an eyebrow, staring at the Dampire. "No, of course not."

The Dampire paced back and forth in front of the Great Wizard's desk. "Then it's of no use to me. I need you to open a portal to my personal domicile so I can gather clothing that will fit me."

"I'm not your handler," Zerron said dismissively. "Have Selandra do it when she recovers. You demanded for her to be present for the mission report. I demand that you leave me be."

"If you're too busy shuffling scrolls around," Xander coyly grinned, "you do have the option of removing the wardings on me so that I may go there myself."

"Out of the question, Master Bane. Now leave me or I will activate your wardings."

Xander slowly walked over to the doorway, but then he paused. Zerron glanced up at the diminutive Dampire and asked, barely able to hide his irritation, "You wish to say more?"

"A quick query." The Dampire turned his head to look back at the Great Wizard. "If a mage goes rogue, can they re-enter Le'orn?"

Zerron tilted his head, eyeing him suspiciously. "No. The warding here will mark them as an outside threat and prevent them from entering. Mages that go rogue are hunted down and executed for their betrayal of the oaths they took. Why do you ask?"

Showing little emotion, Xander shrugged. "No reason." And then he teleported away.

Chapter Eight

Late the next day, Selandra woke up, feeling lethargic and upset. Tears escaped from her bleary eyes as she rubbed the area on her neck that her partner drank from. It was painfully raw, just like her emotional state. She turned her head to see if he was lying next to her and immediately regretted it. Pain flared from her neck, like someone slipped a blade into the muscles.

The mage's breaths came in rapid succession. She bit her bottom lip as the wave of pain finally subsided. She gingerly turned and looked at her bed and then searched the room for her partner. No sign of the Dampire but on her nightstand was a tray of food and several glasses of orange juice. She sat down on the side of the bed and noticed a folded piece of parchment.

Selandra sipped on her juice as she unfolded and read the letter.

Dearest Sel,

Please eat and drink up. It will help you feel better after what I put you through. Know that I meant what I said. Never make demands when it comes to blood. I can't be your partner if you force me to do things that I don't want.

X.

"You bastard," Selandra muttered as she stood up and walked over to her closet. She opened the closet to retrieve a new outfit and found Xander sleeping on the floor. He seemed to be fitfully sleeping, curled up in a fetal position, clutching one of the mage's cloaks.

Emotions warred in her mind as she watched him, stroking her neck unconsciously. Despite what he did to her last night, Selandra still cared about the diminutive Dampire. The mage quietly reached down and retrieved her boots and tugged them on.

She put her hands on her hips and kicked his prone body several times, snarling, "Wake up, bastard! Get the hell up!"

He didn't budge, only grunted, which caused Selandra to kick harder and faster.

"Get up and face me, you jerk!" she blurted out in between her angry sobbing. "Get up, damnit!"

The mage felt light-headed and dropped down hard on her knees, holding herself up with her palms on the floor, panting from exertion. Sweat beaded on her face as she heard Xander calmly ask, "Are you done?"

"I need..." Selandra's anger flared, "my staff... and I will... show you...no mercy..."

Xander remained unmoving, his eyes still closed. "You're right. I don't deserve mercy. Not from you. Not from anyone."

"Get up so we can have a proper confrontation," the Peacekeeper hissed as she reached out and smacked the Dampire on his shoulder with a balled fist. Selandra's other arm gave way and she collapsed on the floor, her tears trickling out unabated.

The mage felt the familiar softness of her cloak as it was draped over her bare skin. She looked up at Xander. He put his hands on her shoulders and teleported them back on the bed. Selandra remained on her stomach as the Dampire swiftly brought her fresh clothes.

"Why haven't you eaten yet?" Xander asked as he sat beside her with the tray of food.

"Why do you care?" the mage bitterly replied, not wanting to look at her partner. "You hurt me."

"This is true, but it serves as the perfect reminder that I'm still a monster."

She turned to look at him, but howled in pain. She grasped the area as the pain spiked in her neck. Xander rolled the mage over, examining her neck with concern and confusion.

"*You* did this to me, you ass!" Selandra barked out.

"I have no clue what you're talking about."

"It hurts...where you...bit me..."

"Hmm," Xander prodded her neck as he scratched his chin. He noticed that her skin was red and hot to the touch. "This isn't right. Something else is happening."

"Fix your fuck up!" Selandra growled, the pain seemed to be getting worse.

"I didn't do this!" the Dampire hissed as he got mere inches from her pain scrunched face. "I'd say keep your panties on, but you're not wearing any. Now stop screaming at me and let me figure out the problem."

"You're my problem," Selandra retorted as she gritted her teeth and squeezed her eyes shut.

Xander ignored her as he palpated the angry patch of skin. The mage tried to swat his probing fingers away, not able to endure the pressure from his touch. The Dampire pinned both her arms to her sides and he straddled her body, keeping her arms in place.

He leaned down and sniffed her neck and was surprised. It wasn't an infection that wafted up, but magic. Before his eyes, a strange sigil rose to the surface. The Dampire's eyes went completely black as he chanted in his demonic tongue, trying to counter the magic, but it wasn't working.

"Someone's torturing you, Sel," Xander stated. She was about to speak, but he cut her off, "Don't accuse me of this! Come! I'll show you in the mirror what's happening to you."

The Dampire teleported them into the bathroom. He held her up and demanded, "Open your damn eyes and see the mark!"

Selandra pried open one of her eyes, she had difficulty seeing through her blurry vision. She rapidly blinked her eyes and managed to make out the symbol. It was three circles in each other. Each one had tendrils slithering out and stabbing into the muscles. Her eyes widened as she ordered, her lips quivering, "Get me to Zerron, NOW!"

"I have no clue where the prick is."

Selandra managed to focus on the Great Wizard, locating him easy enough, and blurted out, "Observatory."

Xander gripped her around her waist tightly and teleported them directly in the observatory, startling the Great Wizard. Xander ordered Zerron with a growl, "Help her!"

"What has happened to her?"

"How should I know," the Dampire retorted as he pointed at her neck. "Someone is hurting her."

He strolled over and examined her neck. His eyes widened as he corrected Xander. "No, someone is killing her. Lie her down, Master Bane."

Selandra's eyes rolled back as she crumbled down to the floor, her body spasmed and jerked wildly. Xander straddled her to hold her flailing body in place so she wouldn't hurt herself.

"Do something about it," the Dampire growled.

Zerron disappeared right before Xander's eyes. He wasn't sure if the Great Wizard was going after the necessary items to counter this magical attack or simply left his partner to die in his arms. It wouldn't surprise him if Zerron chose the latter.

The leader of the Peacekeepers of Le'orn had proven that he's untrustworthy in the Dampire's mind. He sent him and his partner on missions that should have had more mages, but the lack of information had also been just as detrimental.

"Stay with me, Sel," Xander spoke, concern etched into his words. "The prick should be back anytime now."

Blood and a strange foam trickled down from the corners of Selandra's mouth. Xander instinctively turned the mage's body on her side and forced her mouth open. As if on cue, Zerron reappeared. He brought with him a small chest. He sat down as Selandra puked out the foam and blood. Zerron pulled out a small crystal and several bottles of powdered herbs.

"Can you fix this?" Xander asked as he tried to keep his partner's hair out of the way of the fluids she was spitting up.

"I'm not sure. It shouldn't be possible for any outsiders to attack us magically unless," Zerron eyed the Dampire and asked, "did someone take a sample of her hair while you two were at Crimson Pass?"

"Not that I'm aware of," Xander answered as Selandra jerked more, "but I may know of someone that might be responsible."

The Great Wizard poured the powdered herbs into his hand. As he muttered an incantation, the crystal glowed brightly. Zerron put his hand directly on the mage's inflamed spot on her neck, sweat causing the powders to adhere to the skin. He placed the crystal on Selandra's temple and muttered once more.

Selandra bowed her chest out and let out a blood curdling howl that caused both Xander and Zerron to flinch. Her eyes were closed tightly as tears of blood trickled down her cheeks.

"It's not working," Zerron said, feeling confused. "Something is amiss. Whoever is doing this to her has managed to counter my work. I can't stop the attack."

"Then I will go fetch him for you," Xander replied as he straightened up. "This is going to be painful so be ready for my return."

"The wardings will snap you back quickly, so I suggest you grab the assailant the moment you see him."

"Break the warding and this could go smoothly," the Dampire stated, his lips curled up in disgust.

"There's no time! She will be dead by then."

Selandra wailed louder as Xander touched her shoulder. "For you, I do this, Sel." He glanced up and commanded, "Be ready to spell him when I return. He's a tricky one."

"Go, then. I'm ready for the culprit."

Xander closed his eyes and thought about Merrick. Everyone has a signature, similar to a calling card, something that the Dampire was able to use to track down his victims over the centuries. It never mattered where they were hiding, Xander found them easily enough.

This time was different. He normally would stalk his intended targets for days, watching their every move. Now, he had to literally grab the conjurer and get painfully sprung back into the spire. Xander decided that, if he could, he was going to bite down on Merrick and drink the mage's off-putting blood.

Xander teleported himself directly onto the conjurer's back. Merrick was holding a small cast iron cauldron in one hand while he used the other to draw energy from the contents within it. The Dampire viciously tore into Merrick's neck as the warding kicked in.

Pain coursed through the Dampire's body, but he was able to dampen it with the *volunteered* blood. The two crashed on the floor, just three feet away from Selandra. Zerron moved swiftly and jerked the cauldron out of Merrick's hands. He placed his hand on the conjurer's forehead and commanded with an angry scowl, "Merrick, sleep!"

Merrick seemed to resist the command, surprising the Great Wizard as he removed his hand. The conjurer grinned as he eyed his former leader, but groaned in pain as the Dampire kept drinking. Zerron glanced down at the contents of the cauldron and sneered. He put a hand up and uttered the phrase, *"Reddere quod ablatum!"*

Merrick screamed as his body went rigid, energy streamed from his body and went into Selandra. Xander pulled his fangs from Merrick's neck and rolled off his back and onto the floor. He curled up in a ball as the warding took hold, like his diminutive body was being crushed under a landslide of boulders.

Merrick's body stilled, but before he lost consciousness, he uttered, "She's mine and no one can have her..."

Zerron raised up fully and twisted his emerald ring on his finger. He walked over to Selandra and saw that she was no longer writhing in pain, just softly whimpering. He kneeled down by the female mage as a door to the observatory burst open. A small cluster of mages poured in as Zerron ordered, "Take Merrick to the enchanted holding room."

"What about these two?" one mage asked as the others bound the conjurer.

"Jasper. You, Hogarth, and Devon wait outside. I need to ensure that Selandra is truly out of danger."

"What exactly did Merrick do to her," Xander croaked out as he stood up, his face scrunched in pain. Zerron was surprised by the fact that the Dampire was standing, let alone speaking.

"You should sit down and rest. The warding I placed on you is-"

"Quite painful and a burden," Xander growled, causing the remaining mages to flinch. His body seemed different to everyone, including Zerron. The tint of his skin got darker and redder, his fangs, as well as his teeth grew longer and sharper. His muscular structure got more pronounced and bulged, making him look larger than normal. The gray claws on both his fingers and toes grew out three inches longer and were black.

He snarled as he walked over to Selandra's weeping body, black blood dripping down from his mouth and chin. "Fix her or you're all next to fall to my bloodlust!"

The mages unsheathed their swords and protectively positioned themselves in front of the Great Wizard. Zerron examined Selandra's neck and stated without looking at the Dampire, "The warding will keep me safe from your assault. Let me do what I can to help your handler."

Xander hissed a laugh that caused everyone, including the Great Wizard to freeze. "Is that a fact? Your wardings might be causing me some discomfort now, but what's a little more pain to endure if it means that I can actually get to rip out your throat?"

Zerron glanced up at the Dampire, his fear grew in light of what Merrick managed to accomplish. A weak voice spoke and said, "Xander? Where's my partner at?"

Xander's menacing glare fell on Selandra. Her eyes were closed, her face covered in her own gore, and her lips were trembling. The Dampire's anger ebbed at the sight of his partner, he could sense that Merrick's death magic had stopped and her heart was beating normally.

"He's here, my child," the Great Wizard cooed. "He's patiently waiting for me to finish with you." He cast a stern look at the Dampire. "He's just worried about you. After all, you are his Bride and it's his duty to ensure that he takes care of you."

As Zerron put his hands on Selandra to magically probe her body, Xander responded. "There's no such thing as a 'Bride' and you know it. Now, fix her up so we may go about our business."

"Why did you hurt me?" Selandra croaked out, barely opening her eyelids to see him, but couldn't because of the other mages around her. "I can't understand why you would put me through this kind of torture."

Xander roared as more pain coursed through his body. "I didn't do this to you! Why must I be the first one everyone suspects of treachery? Is she fixed or not?"

Zerron stood up gracefully and bristled as he replied, "Selandra is well, but I meant what I said. You need to take care of her. She was having her life force stolen from her by Merrick. I, for one, would like to know how he's still alive when the team of mages that went with him on their mission claimed to have witnessed his demise."

Xander didn't care as he motioned for the mages to stand aside, but they didn't budge, so he stated, flashing his monstrous grin. "Let me take her now or do you three wish to do the dance of death with me?"

"Xander is no longer a threat," Zerron stated as he walked around the mages. He placed his hand on the Dampire's shoulder and squeezed. "Are you, Xander?"

"I am and always will be a threat," the Dampire replied. "No matter where I go, no matter who I'm with. I shall always be a threat because I'm a *monster*. An *abomination*!"

"Shut up, Xander." Selandra weakly snapped, "You're an ass, not a monster. How many times do I have to say it before it takes hold?"

"You wouldn't say that if you could see me in my current form," the Dampire answered bitterly, looking away in shame.

"Take your Bride back to her room," Zerron stated. "Once she is able, I want to know everything that transpired and what you know about Merrick."

The mages sheathed their weapons and parted so Xander could get to his partner, but each one had a hand on the hilts. Xander bent down and effortlessly lifted the mage up. She curled up in his arms as she opened her eyes fully, noting that he refused to look at her. She saw what he meant by being a monster, yet it didn't frighten her. She strained to lift her arm up and caressed his cheek briefly before her limb dropped helplessly down to her lap.

"Look at me, Xander," Selandra pleaded, and then added, "Please?"

Begrudgingly, he complied. His eyes were as black as obsidian and his regal face seemed disproportionately larger. The mage could feel the difference in his muscles, they seemed firmer and more pronounced. Selandra weakly giggled to herself, wondering if other areas of his massive physique grew.

"What's so funny, woman," Xander barked. "Does my demonic side amuse you?"

"More like intrigued by what other parts of you have grown." Selandra smirked and wiggled her eyebrows suggestively.

The Dampire looked over at the Great Wizard and commanded, "Put her to sleep like you did to me, but only long enough to recover from this attack."

"I will, but I need to hear about your mission first. With what just transpired today, I want to know everything," Zerron answered and then commanded the other mages to leave. They all bowed in unison before marching out, which made Xander roll his eyes. A plush couch materialized behind the Dampire and a plush wingback chair appeared before the Great Wizard.

Xander sat down, still holding his partner in his arms. He didn't want to do this now, but Zerron did promise to let Selandra sleep afterwards. It finally dawned on her what they agreed to. "Hey! I'd like a say in this matter. I don't need to be rendered unconscious! I'm fully capable of recovering on my own."

"Then report your findings and I may consider it," Zerron replied with little emotion.

Xander looked down at the mage and said, "Fine. I will talk about Crimson Pass if you can fill him in on the parts I missed out on, with Merrick. Agreed?"

Selandra nodded.

"To be blunt, you've been screwed, Zerron. The vampires of Crimson Pass have formed an alliance with the necromancer. The threat of Le'orn is gone and they've been drinking from sentient beings that she has ensnared with her magic in order to buy their support. A type of loophole to get around the Vampire Pact."

"This necromancer is building an army," Zerron muttered to himself as he stroked his chin, concern etched in his face. He looked at the Dampire and asked, "What else?"

"They tried to kill us. I'm sure that comes as no surprise to you. They gave Sel enough leeway to see the council after imprisoning us. We escaped, both the dungeon and Crimson Pass, but a horde of reanimated corpses chased after us."

"How did they know where you two went? I imagine that you portaled far away."

"I had a tracking spell placed on me by..." Xander paused for a moment, wondering if he should reveal his relationship with Vestal, instead said, "One of the council members. He seemed adamant that we should not make it back here alive to tell our tale."

"I see," Zerron answered solemnly. "How does Merrick fit into this?"

"I took the tracker back to the vile enclave. I noticed small rifts that allowed the dead to come through. They were definitely coming from Crimson Pass and I managed to snatch the dead horde's puppeteer. I brought Merrick to Sel for questioning. I was surprised that she knew him. I will let her tell the rest."

"What did you glean from Merrick?" Zerron asked, concealing his ire, yet Xander felt it.

"He's in league with the necromancer because she brought him back to life. He tried to sway me to join him, but I refused. He managed to use some powerful magic on us both." She looked up at the Dampire as a tear escaped down her cheek. "He nearly killed Xander by impaling him with some nasty life leeching roots. He wanted to take Xander's head off, which he almost accomplished, so he could give it to me, as a trophy."

"Why would he do this?"

"I...I'd rather not go into full details-"

"Yes, you *will*," Zerron admonished as he steepled his fingers together. "We have enemies surrounding us and *you* want to skip over details? Details that could mean the difference between life or death?"

Xander pointed an accusatory clawed finger at the Great Wizard, smirking. "You taught her well, I'd say. You do it all the time. It's quite burdensome when the roles are reversed, isn't it?"

Zerron ignored the Dampire and commanded, "Speak, Selandra."

"He was making claims." The mage glanced up at Xander, then back at Zerron. "Merrick said that he knew who slaughtered my parents during the Fae war. He practically accused Xander of the crime, but never outright said it. I believe he was trying to pit us against each other."

"He wasn't a part of the Fae war. How could he possibly know this?"

"He's learned the art of necromancy and claimed to have summoned my mother..."

Selandra choked up at the thought of Merrick desecrating her mother's eternal resting place, "and asked her himself. He's obsessed over me for some reason and thinks that if he kills my parent's killer that I will be with him. He's gone mad from the dark magic."

"I see," Zerron flatly stated as he looked between the two. "Is there anything else either of you wish to tell me?"

"The people that are going missing can be found at Crimson Pass," Xander answered as he shifted out from under his partner. Selandra looked over at him and noticed that his demonic side was receding, but not by much. Her eyes widened when she caught a glimpse of his member. It had grown bigger than normal.

"They're pretty much dead and yet, still alive, which is how the vampire council is able to skirt around the Vampire Pact and have fresh blood donors. Unless the necromancer is using these people in other ways, it's the only answer we have for you. Just know, the council doesn't fear this place and have declared war on you and any aligned with Le'orn," Xander said matter of fact.

Zerron stood up as he ordered, "Go now and rest. That means you, Selandra. If it's a war they want, then we all need to be prepped, rested and ready. I fear darker days are on the horizon that could make the Fae war look like a minor dispute."

The Dampire cocked an eyebrow. "Unless you were there, you know nothing of that war. Come Sel, we both need a change of scenery," he motioned to himself and at her and grinned, "and new wardrobes."

Chapter Nine

He teleported them back to her bed. Xander looked at Selandra and told her, "Get dressed. I need to do something about *this*."

"What do you mean?"

He snarled as he teleported away, leaving the mage alone. Selandra got off the bed and slowly walked over to the closet. A mortifying thought occurred to the mage as she grabbed her clothes.

I was skyclad in front of the Great Wizard Zerron and other Peacekeepers!

Selandra quickly slipped on her purple tunic and snatched her cloak off the floor and strolled back to her bed. She pulled her boots off and put on skin-tight leather pants. The Peacekeeper secured her sword and staff to her attire and then she rummaged through the Dampire's tattered pile of clothes and grabbed his money bag. Selandra tied it to her belt and walked back to the bed. The mage put her purple cloak on just as Xander reappeared.

He appeared to have reverted back to his normal state, despite looking more disheveled than when he left. Selandra wondered what the Dampire had to do to satisfy his demonic side.

"So where did you have in mind for the change of scenery," Selandra asked as Xander teleported onto her back. He inhaled deeply and groaned happily, which made the Peacekeeper nibble on her lip.

"My place. If it hasn't escaped those piercing, all-seeing eyes of yours, I'm still in need of clothes. Do you know where it's at?"

Selandra closed her eyes, searching and then replied, "Yes, I can feel it."

Xander teleported them to their spot by the lake and hopped down to the ground without making a sound. The Peacekeeper held her staff, the tip of the crystal pulsating, as she muttered an incantation with her arm extended. In moments, a portal coalesced before them. Selandra looked down at the Dampire and said, "I think I've opened a portal to your personal domicile, but with everything that's transpired thus far, I'm doubting myself and my abilities."

Xander shrugged his little shoulders as he spoke. "Not to worry. If you missed it, it doesn't reflect on your abilities. I have enchantments in place to conceal it, but I'm sure that it can't deceive *my* Peacekeeper."

"No matter which answer awaits on the other side, I'll never know for sure," Selandra huffed, her frustration obvious.

"This is true, so let's see just how bad it is," Xander quipped as he walked through the portal, grinning ear to ear.

"Bastard," the Peacekeeper muttered. She took a deep, calming breath and stepped through. Selandra saw an old fortress upon exiting her portal. There was nothing spectacular about the dilapidated structure, it appeared to be in disarray and in dire need of repairs. The mage wondered if Xander took over this place during the Fae war, the ravages of magical assaults on its outer walls showed scorching signs of battle.

She glanced at the Dampire with a questioning look. "You chose *this* as your home?"

"Yes, I did."

"Willingly?"

Xander grinned as he grasped the mage's hand and walked forward. "Come, Sel. There's more to this than you think."

Selandra had her doubts. It gave off the impression of a tomb from warfare. The mage felt her skin tingling all over her body and a strong desire to flee. Her vision was assaulted by the decaying visages of dead warriors, screaming at her.

Xander gently squeezed her hand and stated, "Stay with me, mage. It will be over in a moment."

Selandra nodded as she closed her eyes, feeling extremely uncomfortable. She felt ethereal hands touching her, trying to force her to let go. The pressure became intense and then, it was gone. The mage opened her eyes and looked around.

No ghosts glared back at her and the tingling sensation was gone. Xander shrugged his little shoulders as the Peacekeeper looked at him. "You mages have your security, I have my own deterrent. Keeps the riff-raff out."

Selandra looked back at the spot where they just stepped through. She outstretched her arm and grazed the barrier. At contact, several spectral faces appeared.

"Is this an illusion or are they real?"

"What do you think?" Xander asked.

"It doesn't feel like any type of illusion that I've ever encountered. Did you seriously trap ghosts here to protect your rundown domicile?"

Xander looked unfazed by her comment. "You say that like it's a bad thing. I merely put the former inhabitants here to good use."

"That's cruel, even for you, Xander," Selandra replied as she took her hand away.

"This is true," the Dampire said. "Trust me when I say that they're not happy about it.

If I hadn't guided you through the barrier, you would be dead and added to the protection."

The mage's mouth gaped at him. "Has that actually happened?"

"Of course, it has. Why do you think it felt so uncomfortable? This fortress has earned a reputation for being a haunted death trap. Anyone that actually makes it through ends up trapped here. Naturally, I feed on them for trespassing." Xander grinned as he motioned to his home. "Shall we, Sel?"

The mage turned and halted as the fortress came into view. The structure appeared to be in immaculate condition. It still had the scorch marks, but the fortress appeared to be solid and battle ready. Xander was amused by her astonished look and said, "Yes, that was an illusion you saw. Do you really think my home would be in such shambles?"

"Anything is possible when it comes to you, Xander."

The Dampire walked ahead and pulled open the heavy oak door and waved his arm inside. "After you, Sel."

Selandra walked in and noticed that every part of the Dampire's fortress was in pristine condition. There wasn't a speck of dust nor any signs of deterioration anywhere. Everything looked brand new and spotless. The Peacekeeper looked at the Dampire, who shrugged. "It's not much to look at, but it works for my needs."

"I'm confused," Selandra said as she examined one of the wooden support beams. "If this is truly a relic from the Fae war, then how is it that this place looks like it was just built yesterday?"

"Use your finely tuned senses and tell me what you see, Sel." Xander grinned as he sat down on a nearby chair. He intently watched the mage as she placed a hand on the stone wall and her other hand on a wooden beam. After a few minutes of probing, Selandra gasped.

"This place was created by pure magic. That can't be right, can it?"

Xander beamed a toothy smile. "If I said it before, I'll say it again; you're a smart mage, Sel."

"But who did it and where did they go?"

"This place was created by pure magic by an eccentric fellow by the name of Dracon. I'm sure in your vast studies you've encountered that name."

"Are you sure? Dracon is a mythical being, said to weld immense power that could level an entire continent. He's just a story, not real."

"Sure, just a legend, but we both know that with all stories comes a certain amount of truth. If Dracon could easily destroy the landscape, what's to say that he couldn't create as well?" Xander replied with a smirk.

Selandra narrowed her eyes at the Dampire, "Do you have some sort of proof or is this a mere jest at my expense?"

"I do. It's all around you, Sel. Who else could've done this?"

"The Great Wizard has this ability," the mage countered, but she felt like something was different here. This place wasn't anything like the spire, magical energy hummed throughout the fortress, as though it were alive.

"This is true, but he used the materials in the environment for his Gods awful phallic palace. This was created from nothing. Just pure magic."

The Dampire teleported himself next to Selandra. He grasped her by the hand and escorted her through the fortress. It had stone stairways that ascended to eight different floors. Each floor was unique and different than the last, according to Xander.

Selandra wasn't quite convinced. Everything about the structure was solid, the craftsmanship impeccable. They strolled up the staircase to the fourth floor. Xander motioned to the only door that seemed out of place. A wooden door that was stained blue and had no visible way of opening it, though there was a small, odd shaped hole that could fit a doorknob. She put her hand on the door and immediately recoiled from it as an angry growl erupted from behind it.

The mage glanced down at the Dampire, "What was that? What do you have trapped in there?"

"I'd tell you, but you wouldn't believe me," Xander replied coyly.

"Whatever it is, it's pissed off."

"Do you want to go inside and meet him?"

"I do, but," Selandra said as she backed away from the door, "I'm not sure that it wants any guests right now."

"This is true," Xander replied with a mischievous grin, "but that has never deterred me from entering."

The Dampire teleported her on the other side of the door. Selandra had difficulty seeing anything or anyone. A threatening deep voice rumbled, echoing in the room. "Why have you come in here? Why bring a female to me? Is she an offering for me to take?"

Selandra snarled, her eyes glowed along with the tip of her staff. "I'm nobody's offering! You come near me and I'll have you crawling away with your head up your ass!"

Dead silence filled the room for a moment before a harsh chuckle filled the air. Selandra could feel its presence all around her and yet, she couldn't pinpoint where this being was exactly.

"A spirited friend of yours, Xander?" the being asked and then added, "I can see that she's special to you. You're bonded with her. I didn't think it was possible."

"Not by choice for either of us," Xander spoke, causing the mage to glare at him, feeling hurt by his statement. "Why would one such as yourself be surprised?"

"Who in their right mind would want to have anything to do with the Abominable Butcher? Clearly, this one has strong feelings for you. I'm surprised that you actually reciprocate this with her. Is this why you're parading skyclad around my room?"

"Who are you and why do you care about me being with him?" Selandra demanded. She felt her anger intensifying, wondering why so many people, including this being, had an issue with her relationship with Xander.

The creature chuckled. "I've been here many ages and never get the company of others. Xander is the first one to stay here and survive with me. He's as much a saint as I am. This is my prison and my name, little lady, is Gerbon."

"Gerbon," Selandra pondered for a moment. "It sounds vaguely familiar. Like I should know it."

Gerbon sighed. "More than likely you've heard more tales of my brother, Dracon. Typical."

The mage wasn't sure what to make of this. "I'm sure that this is some form of a jest at my expense. If this is true, then you would have to be-"

"As old as creation itself. I should know because I was there. I'm not worth knowing, obviously since everyone knows all about my brother. None speak of me?"

"Where's a torch? I want to see you for myself," Selandra said, her eyes barely adjusting to the darkness.

"There isn't one," Xander answered. "If you want to, use your staff, but go slow with the light. He doesn't care much for it."

The Peacekeeper pulled her staff out and let the crystal tip glow just enough ambient light to see the Dampire. He smiled as the light grew bright enough that she could see all around the tiny room. There was only a single chair and a wooden crate that sat next to the far wall. There were no windows or doors, not even the blue door on the other side of the wall. The wall had two stone eyes gazing directly at the mage as a mouth formed before her unbelieving eyes. "This is my form. Are you frightened?"

Selandra stuttered, "Ah, n-no. I-I'm more surprised. What happened to you?"

Gerbon looked down at the diminutive Dampire and said, "She's a fool that knows not how to be afraid. It's obvious because she's in your company."

"What's that remark supposed to mean?" Selandra glared.

Xander cocked his head to the side. "This is true, but she's been forced to be with me. Trust me, you'll find no one more courageous and brilliant than Selandra here."

"That will be her downfall, I fear," Gerbon said sadly.

"Thanks," Selandra huffed. "Sounds like you both have the same opinion about our relationship."

"Xander Bane is wicked and cruel, much like myself. Why risk your life to be bound to a *monster*?"

"As I said, it wasn't her choice in the matter. Her glorious mage leader meddled and created a bond between us."

"Hmm." Gerbon thought for a moment and then ordered, "Both of you, step closer. I want to see if it's true or not."

Selandra and the Dampire got at least two feet away from the ethereal face on the wall. The mage only glared, feeling like she was a horse being prepped for an auction. Gerbon's eyes pulsated and shimmered as he probed the two companions.

"Interesting bond, indeed," Gerbon said. He brought his attention squarely on the Dampire and asked, "Is this meddler the one that placed the enchantments on your person?"

"Yes. For some reason, Zerron doesn't trust me. I have to work for him and Sel here is my handler. The wardings can be restrictive at times," Xander replied with a knowing smirk.

"I can tell from looking at it. You didn't have them when we last spoke. What misdeeds did you do to earn this punishment?" the ethereal face asked.

"He broke the Vampire Pact and now he's in servitude to the Great Wizard," Selandra stated as she looked down at her partner. "I'm the one that's supposed to keep him out of trouble."

Gerbon chuckled loudly. "A full time job I would call it. I'm surprised that he hasn't killed you yet."

"I've warned them both, but neither seem to listen," Xander answered. He looked directly at the mage and added, "She deserves someone better. Someone that will make her happy. That someone isn't me. All I'll do is bring pain and death."

"The Dampire is correct. He will one day be the death of you. Between now and then, only pain will be a part of this path you're on now," Gerbon stated with little remorse.

Selandra rolled her eyes. "If that's what my life will be with Xander, then I accept it. He can try and push me away, but the little imp doesn't understand. I love him as my partner and as his *Bride*."

Xander snorted. "I *told* you that there's no such thing as a Bride for vampires. If there were, there would be sappy romance tales and poems flooding our world."

"Just because it doesn't exist doesn't mean that it isn't possible. You may be right, but what if you're the *first* vampire in history to have a Bride?" Selandra replied as she set her steely gaze on Gerbon. "You never did answer my question. What occurred that would justify this form of imprisonment?"

Gerbon blinked several times before saying, "Surely you jest? My brother, the way he is, should've been boasting about it to the masses. Dracon did love an audience of admirers."

As the Peacekeeper shook her head, Xander confidently spoke to Gerbon with a smirk. "I would say that I'm above telling folks 'I told you so', but that would be a lie."

Confused, Selandra asked, "What are you talking about?"

"He didn't believe me when I told him the same thing. No stories, no epic poems or cautionary tales. This world knows nothing about him, let alone that he exists," the Dampire replied, casting a knowing look at the ethereal face. "Sel didn't know of you until now. That's all you need to confirm what I told you."

"There's only the creation story and Dracon's role in it. A few cautionary tales, but none mentioning you," the mage said as she shrugged.

Gerbon snarled, causing the little room to shake. "That bastard! It wasn't good enough to imprison me. He wanted me wiped from everyone's thoughts! Unleash me so I can right this wrong!"

"As much fun as that would be," Xander answered, "I can't at this time. I'd enjoy seeing the havoc that will follow."

"If you release me," Gerbon tempted the Dampire, "I can rid you of those burdensome wardings. I recognize the magic and I know how to break them. A fair trade, wouldn't you agree?"

Selandra looked down at the diminutive Dampire and hesitantly asked, "Um, do you know why he's been imprisoned like this. I know how much you hate the wardings, but for someone to be trapped in this state can't be good."

"Come now, Xander," Gerbon said, completely ignoring the mage's concern, "we both know that it's what you desire; to be free from any and all obligations. You wouldn't need a chaperone any more. Free me so that I can free you."

"A sound argument you make, Gerbon," Xander replied as he held Selandra's gaze. "He's always looking for ways out of this little predicament that he's in. Nothing was worth the effort, until now. Do you want to know what his crime was that got him locked up?"

As Selandra nodded warily, Xander ordered, "You heard the lady. Tell her your story and don't leave anything out. *Maybe*, and that's a huge maybe, together we can undo what's been done. Is this agreeable, Sel?"

"And I'd like to know if I'm releasing a terrible force on the land," the mage added.

Gerbon chuckled. "She might be a fool for being with you, Xander, but she's also wise to be wary. I'm not going to claim innocence. I did what I did and I don't regret it. My brother and I travelled together. Always wanting something that would help pass the time because being immortal can be dull. Dracon got the brilliant idea to create all that you see before you. The land, the mountains, the sky, and all the life that struggles to survive. We took turns creating animals, but when it came to humans, that was a grave mistake."

"How so," Selandra asked, feeling both confused and irritated. "Are you saying that humanity was a failure? That I'm some sort of mistake?"

"Patience, young lady," the imprisoned immortal replied. "Leave all queries you have until I finish the tale. Just for the record, you're not a mistake, just naive for being with Xander. Now, where was I?"

"Humanity is a piss pot in your eyes," Xander replied.

"Right," Gerbon said. "My brother thought it would be a brilliant idea to create bipedal creatures with an intelligence to tend their surroundings and care for the beauty we created together. It didn't take long for them to show their true nature. There was no harmony to be had. Nothing but stupidity and destruction. Dracon couldn't care less because they sing songs praising him, but I decided that a certain amount of balance was needed so I tweaked humanity secretly and created other races that could rival the humans."

Xander stroked the mage's back. "Gerbon gave magic to humans because it was needed to fight off his magical beings. This is why you have your magical talents, Sel."

Selandra gasped, but held her tongue. She looked down at the diminutive Dampire and mentally asked, *"Are you saying that he made all the other races? Why would he do that?"*

"I did it because it was needed," Gerbon answered as if he read her mind, which Selandra believed that the immortal did. "You have to understand that nature needs tending and since humanity wasn't doing it, I had to create beings that would. This upset my brother deeply because he had no say in the matter. His ire was understandable, but I kept going. All non-human sentient beings in the world are here because I made it so. Dracon felt it necessary to force me to stop so we fought and, if you didn't surmise already, he won. Not because he's stronger than me, but because I couldn't bring myself to hurt him. He reasoned that my tampering with humanity and my own creations hurt him more than any physical attack. I'm the reason for the current state of the world. You may speak, child. I know that you have an inquisitive mind."

"Am I considered human or one of your creations?" the Peacekeeper asked.

Gerbon focused his gaze on Selandra, examining her, which made her feel uncomfortable. "Interesting. I've not seen any of my creations in a long time. I must say that you are a fine specimen."

"What does that mean?"

"It means that you're more than I could've dreamed. I never knew how the seeds of my labor played out, but you've surpassed all my expectations."

Selandra narrowed her eyes. "That didn't answer my question."

"Human. Non-human. What does it matter? In the long run, you're unique and special. That's all that matters and I couldn't be any prouder."

"He's a God, Sel, and this is the price he's paying for making you have magical abilities," Xander interjected, sensing her frustration with Gerbon.

"I wouldn't consider myself a God, but if it helps you cope, so be it." Gerbon chuckled.

Chapter Ten

Selandra stepped forward and put her hand on the wall. She felt a strange wave of magical energy flowing from the immortal and his bindings. Xander eyed the mage intently, but said nothing. She gasped as she recoiled her hand and said, "I don't understand. The bindings are easy to break, even for someone as powerful as you. Why haven't you done it?"

"This is my punishment and I accept it."

Xander spoke up. "He requires an outside assistant for it to work. Dracon made it this way to keep him from escaping."

"This is why I keep asking the little Dampire to do it. I agreed with this form of imprisonment, but after hearing your ignorance of my existence, I feel that I must be released and confront my brother."

Xander took Selandra by her hand and said, "One day you'll be free, but it's not today. Come Sel, let's go to my personal chamber. I'm in need of fresh clothing. Plus, there's more to show you."

The Dampire teleported them directly into a long corridor. Everything about this place was immaculate and in pristine condition, just like the other areas the Peacekeeper had seen. The stone walls had gold sconces seamlessly attached, lighting their way by using orbs of magical energy. There were doors on either side of the corridor.

Xander stopped by a black metal door and stated as he lifted the handle, "This is my personal chamber in this place."

The black door swung open, revealing a large king-size bed with four corner posts. There was an ornately crafted armoire on the opposite side of the room, next to another doorway. Selandra stepped in and looked up at the ceiling and saw that it had a large crystal chandelier hanging down, lighting the room with the same type of energy orbs.

Xander walked over to the armoire and opened the double doors, revealing a complete wardrobe for his size. Selandra sat down on the edge of the bed, watching the Dampire as he reached for some clothes. She smiled, taking in his muscular form as they flexed with each movement.

"If you keep eye fucking me, Sel," Xander said as he looked over his shoulder at the mage, "I might be tempted to return the favor, but not with my eyes."

"Like I would stop you. You're a bastard Xander Bane, but you're also *my* bastard."

The Dampire grumbled under his breath as he bent over, making sure to give the mage a full view of his bare ass. He chuckled at the sound of her appreciative breath she let out. Xander slipped on a crimson tunic with a hunter green vest and form fitting black pants. He turned around and walked over to the bed, carrying a pair of ankle boots and a black leather jacket similar to the one that was destroyed.

As he sat down on the edge of the bed, Selandra said, "Can I ask you something?"

The Dampire grinned as he tugged one of his boots on. "You just did."

"I'm being serious," the Peacekeeper huffed.

"So was I." Xander cackled as she smacked him on the shoulder. He tugged on the other boot and added, "What is it that you wish to know?"

"Why live all alone in this place?"

"I'm not alone. I have Gerbon here to keep me company," Xander replied as he slipped off the bed.

He put his leather jacket on as Selandra asked, "Maybe so, but why here, of all places? Surely, there's better places in the capital that would have sufficed."

The Dampire adjusted his garments and eyed the Peacekeeper incredulously. "Why are you asking questions that you already know the answer to, Sel?"

"I want to know you better, that's all. If I'm to be your-"

"Don't you dare say *Bride*, there's no such thing," Xander hissed, interrupting her. The mage flinched, as though wounded by his words. Xander sighed as he walked over and stood between her spread legs. He put his hands on her thighs and said, "I'm a monster, Sel, we've had this discussion. No one wants to live where an evil fiend lives next door to them. I've tried through the centuries, before and after the war. It's ironic that people fear me, but have no problem being subjugated to the ruling Fae of all the realms. They might have won the war, but I'm sure that I was on the right side of the fight. It doesn't matter where I go, I'll always be an outcast and reviled."

"I don't see you that way, Xander."

"The events that have transpired since our paths crossed says otherwise. You're now just as much an outcast as I am. The only difference is that I've had time to accept it. You don't deserve it."

The mage kneeled down and put her arms around Xander's diminutive form. "If I'm to be an outcast, why not learn from the best. I don't know why you keep trying to push me away. I really wish that you would stop it."

The Dampire sniffed Selandra's scent as he nuzzled his face in her breasts. He looked up at her with one eye open and replied, "I do it because I feel that our relationship was forced upon us both. I do it because you deserve a life. A better life that I can't give you without destroying all that you worked so hard to achieve."

"Do you feel nothing for me?" Selandra asked. Xander noticed that she was holding her breath and her heart rate had increased.

"Let me pose a question to you: if Zerron hadn't done what he did, would you still be pining for me? If we ran into each other at one of the local pubs, what would you have done?"

The Peacekeeper's lips parted as Xander added, "You don't need to answer. Just think about it. Come along, Sel. Make a portal and let's go rest before we go after the necromancer."

Selandra nodded in agreement. Fatigue was creeping over her body as she stood up. The mage extended her arm and muttered the incantation, creating a portal back to Le'orn. Xander teleported himself on her back as she walked through. The lake shimmered in the moonlight; the magical energy pulsated in it as though the body of water was alive.

The mage's legs buckled slightly, but she kept her balance. Xander muttered next to her ear, causing the mage to shiver, "Hold on, Sel. I'll get us back to your room."

"Don't you mean *our* room," Selandra corrected him.

"I'm not certain that I can say that just yet. Not after the way I treated you."

"That was my fault. I never knew that a vampire's bloodlust could be so- "

"Dangerous?"

"Cruel," the mage said. She caught a glimpse of regret in his eyes and the slight grimace. Selandra could tell that her wording for the act hurt him. "Please promise me that you won't hurt me again like that. I know that I got what I deserved because of my ignorance. Will you guide me so I can learn more about vampires so I don't make a fatal mistake?"

"I'll tell you everything that I know, I promise you. But not now. Let's go to your bed, if you'll have me," the Dampire replied as he teleported them directly to the mage's quarters. Before the mage could say anything, Xander removed her cloak and weapons. Xander walked around to face his haggard mage and pulled her towards the bed. He sat Selandra down on the edge and then he took off both of her boots at once.

The Dampire glanced up at the Peacekeeper and commented as he slipped his nimble fingers around the waistband of her pants, "No protesting the monster that's getting you ready for bed?"

Selandra half-heartedly shrugged. "I'm too exhausted to care. I don't want to argue with you about taking care of me."

"Good girl." The Dampire chuckled as he tugged her pants down, letting them pool at her ankles. "You're a treasure that any man should cherish. You deserve a little pampering every now and then."

The mage kicked her pants away as Xander appeared behind her. He tugged her tunic up as the mage held her arms up. "You still believe that you're not good enough to be that man?"

"Think about it," Xander replied as he pulled her back further up the bed. "How much pain and suffering have you had to endure because you were forced to be my handler? Several times you've nearly died. Is that the fairy tale life that you want to have with me?"

As the Dampire crawled over to her side, the mage replied, "I admit that my time with you has been an interesting whirlwind of chaos, but that's to be expected for a Peacekeeper of Le'orn." She lifted her hips up to make it easier for Xander to take her panties off. "I'd gladly lay my life down for you because I'm just expendable like that, at least in Zerron's eyes."

Xander looked at her as she laid there with her eyes closed, her head turned to the side. Selandra felt him leave her side, but refused to open her eyes. The void from Xander's absence made her heart ache. Selandra wondered if the Dampire was right about their relationship. *Would I treat him differently? Is my heart playing tricks on me? Without the bond, would Xander want me?* The weight shifted on the bed, letting her know that Xander had returned. She figured that he had put her clothing away for her. He pulled the covers up and over their bodies as he cuddled up next to her. The mage smiled as she felt his bare skin against hers.

"My sweet little Sel," Xander purred as he caressed her cheek softly. "Do you truly believe that or did Zerron order you to do so?"

"Yes, to both. You're my number one priority. The Great Wizard covets having you here and will do everything in his power to keep you here as a personal weapon. I'm just a pawn to be sacrificed for the greater good."

"A bunch of rubbish," the Dampire bit out with disgust."

"So, you say, but I'm not even worthy to wield an energy blade." Selandra sighed as she turned her head and opened her eyes, tears trickled down as she added, "The fact that he granted one to you speaks volumes. How can I stop you when you're wielding a weapon so deadly? My weapons are useless against it. You could kill me easily."

"This is true," Xander replied as he leaned in and kissed her cheek, "but that reflects on Zerron as a leader, not you. The man doesn't see you the way that I do. You stopped me back in that tavern when we first met. That alone makes you worthy of such a weapon. Hmm. If you want my knowledge, then I want to know everything Zerron ordered you to do with me."

"It's a deal. As for the energy blade, the Great Wizard may never grant me one. I'm grateful that you have it. We might not be alive without it," Selandra replied as she turned fully on her side to face the Dampire, enjoying his nude form. "It may not mean much but thank you. I feel more like a novice when I compare myself to you."

"Why would you do that?" Xander asked as he brushed a strand of her crimson hair behind her ear. "You're better at many things than me. Things that I can't do properly. Don't tear yourself apart like this. We each have our own unique skill sets that make us both formidable beings, but together, we're an unstoppable team."

Before Selandra could protest, Xander pressed his lips firmly against hers. The mage's tension melted away as she pulled him into a lover's embrace. The Dampire could feel her greedy little tongue probing, searching for a way in. Selandra rolled on her back, pinning the Dampire against her body. Xander shifted his legs until they were directly over the mage's core. The Dampire stroked his thighs against Selandra's core, causing her to moan and squirm. She dug her nails into the Dampire's back. "Wicked little man."

"I do enjoy making my mage squirm," Xander replied as he suckled on each of her breasts. "I'd bite you but-"

"But? Why don't you want to?"

The Dampire leaned forward and kissed her lips as he murmured, "Your body has gone through a lot of trauma. I don't want to needlessly add to it."

Selandra turned her head, exposing her carotid artery. "If we're going to rest for a few days, I want it to start off as pleasurable as possible. Besides, you need to feed."

Xander was hesitant, but the mage eyed him sadly, which caused him to sigh. "Fine, but stop pouting. You're melting my cold, dead heart."

"Shut up and drink me, my Dampire," the mage said. Xander nuzzled her neck, slowly licking her skin. A slight pop and Selandra gasped, smiling as the Dampire drank. He pushed his hips between her thighs and meticulously rubbed his throbbing member against the entrance of the mage's core, teasing her even more.

"Oh Xander," Selandra whimpered. "Take me now! I want you inside me!"

Xander chuckled as he took his fangs out of her neck. "As you wish, Sel."

Xander leaned back on his knees and lifted Selandra's legs up in the air. He rested them against his shoulders, still gyrating his member at the mage's slick folds. Gently, the Dampire pushed his member inside, causing the mage to moan. Xander steadily increased his speed, allowing Selandra time to acclimate to his girth. The mage bucked her hips, trying to match his rhythmic thrusts.

"Oh, Xander," Selandra cried out. "Mmmm. Go deeper."

Xander hoarsely replied, "All in due time."

"Please," the mage pleaded, wanting to fill her core completely. "I want you to do it now."

"Fine," the Dampire said with a mischievous smirk. "I'll humor you, but first, I want to try something with you."

The mage looked at Xander as he licked the back of her left calf methodically. She bit her bottom lip, anticipating his bite. His eyes locked with hers as he asked, "Are you ready, my love?"

"Yes, Xander," Selandra bit out, wondering what he was planning. Xander lifted her legs off of his shoulders and pushed them together. His fangs punctured the mage's calf slowly as he leaned forward, her thighs were touching her belly. Selandra could feel that her core was tighter in this position, which made Xander's member feel bigger.

The Dampire pushed inside the mage as far as he could and then his thrusting increased with vampiric speed. Selandra moaned loudly as she arched her back. She did her best to keep up with the Dampire's speed, which seems impossible to do. The mage's breathing came in short, shallow gasps as her eyes rolled back in her head.

Xander removed his fangs and licked the puncture wounds, but didn't cease the speed of his thrusting. He could feel Selandra's wet core constricting around his pulsating member. Xander greedily ordered, "That's it, Sel. Come for me!"

"Like I..." Selandra replied, panting breathlessly as sweat glistened all over her body, "have a... choice..."

At that moment, the mage cried out as an orgasmic wave cascaded throughout her entire body. Selandra's eyes glowed as her body spasmed. She dug her nails into the Dampire's back as she felt his member swelling. Xander grunted and growled as his member shot jets of hot ejaculation inside Selandra's dripping core. He sat there on his knees; his weight being supported by the mage's legs.

Xander let go of her legs and let them drop down on the mattress as he laid down on top of Selandra, breathing hard. He grinned at his mage and asked, "Was that fast and deep enough to satisfy your core's insatiable hunger for me?"

Selandra's head felt like it was in a fuzzy haze, as she muttered, "W-What?"

Xander chuckled. "I'll take that as a yes."

The Dampire pulled himself off of the mage and covered her up. Selandra felt him leave her bed, which made her instinctively reach out for him. Her entire body shook and felt too heavy to move. Xander climbed back into the bed and slid underneath the covers. He eyed the mage closely and said, "Sleep well, Sel. You're going to need it for the next few days."

"But," Selandra replied as her head lulled to the side, "the mission?"

"It can wait. You've been through much and need to recuperate. I'll see to it that we're not disturbed, Sel."

The mage nodded half-heartedly and softly snored as she fell fast asleep. Xander draped his little arm across her chest and followed suit.

Chapter Eleven

For nearly two weeks, Xander didn't allow the Peacekeeper to leave her room, despite her many protests. The Dampire told her that since she had her life force magically drained, being physically attacked, and from his feedings, her body needed the downtime. The Dampire brought her plenty of food and wine every day.

Xander had went as far as placing a piece of parchment on the outside of the door that read:

Do not disturb. I don't care who you are or what you want. This is our rest time. If disturbed, you'll find yourself being embraced by my fangs. I will drink you dry without a second thought...

Selandra sat on the side of the bed, rubbing her neck. She felt well enough to take a chance at getting dressed on her own. The Dampire was nowhere in sight, which meant he was probably off to gather more food and wine. Slowly she walked across the room to the closet and saw that the door was left open. The Peacekeeper smiled as she grabbed a purple cloak, a black tunic with matching black leather pants, her calf high boots, underwear, and her weapons.

She felt refreshed, something that the mage hadn't felt since before Xander's arrival in Le'orn. Selandra turned around, happy that her closet was full once more with her stuff, and walked back over to the bed and quickly got dressed. The Dampire refused to let her wear anything, reasoning that it would keep her sequestered easier since she didn't like being seen skyclad around the other mages. He even went so far as emptying out her closet of every article of clothing.

By the time she was dressed, Xander appeared in the room. He looked her over and commented, "Damn. I was getting used to you being skyclad every day."

"Only because you hid my clothes," Selandra countered. "I take it that I'm free to leave our room, since my closet is back to normal?"

"This is true. You're well enough to fend for yourself. " Xander smirked as he added, "About bloody time."

Selandra pointed at the Dampire as she stood up. "You're the one that insisted on keeping me locked up like a damsel in distress." She walked towards the door, opening it with a flick of her fingers, and sheepishly asked with concern as they walked out together, "I wasn't *that* bad off...was I?"

As they walked down the corridor, Xander replied. "More so than you realize. You were practically at death's door. If you kept going, your body would have shut down, which wouldn't be ideal if we ended up in one of the many battles we've been going through already. I...I didn't want to lose you, Sel."

The mage smiled warmly as she pulled her hood up over her head. "What do you say that we go to Herrosa and talk to the monarchy about their little necromancer problem?"

Xander teleported himself on the mage's back as he replied, "That's the plan. Onward, my fair steed. To the lake!"

"I'm not a damn horse!" Selandra hissed.

"I'm not certain of that. I do enjoy riding you in many ways." The Dampire chuckled next to her ear. The mage rolled her eyes as her cheeks heated up. They marched down the long staircase, nodding as the duo passed the other mages who refused to acknowledge either of them. Xander couldn't help flash his fangs, which made a few uncomfortable and was pure entertainment for him.

Selandra went straight for the entrance, but was stopped by Serrock. The massive mage towered over them with his arms across his barrel chest and a sneer on his visage. "I see the blood whore has decided to come out of her room. Why the Great Wizard allows this, I'll never know."

"Zerron could tell you that," Xander answered as he gripped Selandra tightly, "but I'm sure that he knows that one as thick and dense as you wouldn't be able to comprehend it. Tell me, how's the legs?"

Serrock roared with rage as he lunged clumsily towards them. Selandra managed to avoid his grasp as she bolted out the entrance. She ran towards the lake as the Dampire hysterically laughed.

"Must you antagonize him?" Selandra hissed as she panted for air.

"Have we just met?"

"Serrock is a powerful mage. One that you shouldn't cross," Selandra warned.

"The man has the intelligence of a block of wood with wood shavings filling the void in his thick skull. I don't fear him and I refuse to bow down to the cretin."

"I'd rather be on his good side," the mage admonished as she stopped by the lake. Xander slipped off of her back as she caught her breath. "If a war is coming, I want to know that I can trust him not to kill me by 'accident' on the battlefield."

"If you're that worried about him," Xander said as he looked in the direction of the spire entrance. Serrock hobbled outside and motioned with his thumb across his thick neck, glaring at them. "I can end the buffoon right here, right now."

"He's not worth the trouble, let alone the chastising that I'll receive for not keeping you under control."

"I've already warned Zerron that if he didn't deal with that man, then I would." Xander chuckled as he added, "I'm the reason that he's gimping around. Just say the word and I'll gladly break every single bone in his body this time."

Selandra shook her head as she created a portal. "Our healers are elite and would have him up and around within a week. Serrock doesn't let offences against him or his clan go."

"How about I pulverize every bone then? Do you think he'll learn his lesson? Never mind, he's too stupid. It would be like hammering a puddle of water to a tree. Futile."

They walked through the portal together in unison. As they came out on the other side, the Dampire said, "Ah, it appears that we're on the outskirts of Herrosa. I believe that it's high time to get a feel for this place and learn a bit more about this necromancer that's vexing us. I'd teleport us there but with everything that has transpired, I'd rather go in cautiously. Who knows what is waiting for us there?"

They walked together down a well-worn road in silence for the next ten minutes. The clatter of coins caught Xander's attention and he asked the mage, "Do you have my money satchel on you?"

"Yes," Selandra replied as she untied it from her belt. "It was the only thing that I could salvage from your tattered clothing."

"Hmm, I was wondering what happened to this." Xander took his money pouch and tied it to his belt and chuckled. "It sounds like Orimus is still on the loose, making me moncy as we speak."

"I'm surprised that you didn't find it when you hid *all* of my clothes. Does he need to be doing that for you? Aren't you well off as it is?"

Xander took her by the hand as they continued to walk. "He brought it upon himself. He broke the rules of the guild and I got the honor of handing out his punishment. It was either pay me with interest what he tried to cheat me or death. I'm well off, as you put it, but it's the principal of the matter. No one wrongs me without consequences."

Just as the city of Herrosa came into view, the fluttering of wings assailed their ears. A small cluster of pixies swarmed around them with their weapons drawn. One of the male pixies held a sharp steel sword inches from the Dampire's eye, hissing as he said, "Halt! That's far enough for the likes of you two. Turn back and leave this place."

Selandra softly squeezed Xander's hand as several pixies had tiny arrows notched, aimed at her eyes, and proclaimed, "We mean you no harm. Let us pass."

"What she means is that she doesn't want to cause problems. I, on the other hand, welcome the challenge that you've thrown down."

"Herrosa doesn't need any more conjurers," the male pixie retorted as he pressed the tip of his blade into Xander's eye, "or vampires for that matter."

"That's why we are here. To see if we can put an end to this necromancer that's vexing this realm because she's made an enemy with the Peacekeeper's of Le'orn."

Several of the pixies spoke softly to each as Xander stated, "Stand down or prepare to die. It's that simple."

The male pixie growled, "You seem to be forgetting who's in charge here!"

"If you don't let us pass," the Dampire answered coldly, "I'll consider you to be one of the necromancer's army, albeit a tiny one. If you don't take that metal splinter out of my eye, I *will* eat you."

"One word from me and the woman dies," the male pixie warned, not backing down. Several of his companions fluttered next to him with concern etched into their tiny visages.

"We can't harm her if she's a Peacekeeper, Doaks. You know that they're the ones keeping the vampires at bay." The female pixie pointed at Selandra and added, "She can pass, but the vampire stays."

As Doaks glanced over at the other pixies, Xander quickly snatched him out of the air and stuffed him into his mouth. The Dampire chewed slowly, eyeing the other pixies as they watched on in horror. The sounds of tiny bones snapping and crunching caused them to cringe, along with Selandra.

Xander pulled Doaks' sword from his eye and smiled, revealing blood-soaked teeth. The Dampire gulped as he picked his teeth and said coldly, "The best thing about you pixies is that you make great snacks, especially on the battlefield. Your miniscule weaponry are perfect toothpicks. They help get rid of those stubborn pieces of wings out from between my teeth. Anyone else care to do the dance of death with me and join Doaks in my belly?"

The pixies fluttered all around the Dampire, unleashing their arrows on him with precision. Xander cackled as the barrage of arrows struck his body, most bouncing off. Selandra rolled her eyes and cast a protective bubble around the pixies, trapping them.

She stood between them and Xander with her hands on her hips. "This needs to stop. We didn't come here looking for a fight."

"I did," Xander replied with a grin.

"Okay, not with the pixies." She looked at the captive Fae and asked, "I'm sorry about what happened to your friend. My partner can be harsh, but he's got a good heart."

"That's debatable after what I saw him do," the female pixie stated as she glared at the Dampire.

"I did warn him to stand down. I was merely defending us both," Xander replied as if it wasn't a big deal. "He threatened my partner and that sealed his fate."

"You didn't have to eat him!" Selandra scolded. "There's better ways to deal with these people."

Xander shrugged slightly. "This is true, but we both have our own methods. Your bubble can hold them so we can have a civil chat. My way gets my point across easily enough. You should try them. Pixies taste both sweet and crunchy."

The pixies fluttered together with their swords out, warily watching the Peacekeeper. Selandra crinkled her nose in disgust. "Be that as it may, I don't make it a habit of eating sentient beings that I come across."

The Dampire bared his blood-soaked fangs. "I do."

"You're a *monster*! Your ilk should've been exterminated when we won the war," one of the pixies hissed.

"Your kind may have won the fight, but the war hasn't truly ended. Many have tried to end me, but none could best the Abominable

Butcher. Please tell me that we can take them with us. Fae blood is so delicious, Sel."

Little gasps escaped from the captive pixies. One flew up and managed to get eye level with the mage and asked, "How can you side with *him*? Do you not know what you're traveling with? Why would the Peacekeepers ally with, of all the vampires in the world, the Abominable Butcher?"

Selandra could see fear and disgust in their tiny visages. She knew that Xander was a brutal killer, but in her heart, the mage understood him better than most. She raised her hand and said, "I'm going to release you. No more attacking. That goes for you too, Xander." The Dampire shrugged his tiny shoulders in agreement, so the mage added, "Will you tell us more about the necromancer and what she's been doing here?"

"Why should we? It's obvious that you can't keep the Abominable Butcher in control. What guarantee can you give us that he won't eat us too?"

Xander smiled coyly. "I've already eaten so you should be safe for the moment. Answer her questions so we all can go our separate ways."

Selandra glared at the Dampire. "Can you leave us alone so I can get the answers we seek? I don't want to be here all day. We have a job to do."

The Dampire eyed her for a moment and then answered. "Five minutes. That's how long I will give you before I return."

One pixie muttered, "We'd rather you leave and never return."

"You're a funny little pixie. That's why I'll eat you last," the Dampire retorted just as he teleported away.

Selandra eyed the pixies intently, the tip of her boot tapped on the ground. "Well? What do you know?"

One pixie flew up and landed on the mage's shoulder. "I will say what I know, but why do you travel with the Abominable Butcher? Are you his blood slave?"

Selandra glared as her cheeks reddened. "Talk, pixie!"

"My name is Flutter and my small clan has been charged with keeping an eye on the movements within this forest. The necromancer has become a blight on our land. Her dark magic is spreading like a terrible disease with no cure. It seems like everyone associated with her corrupts anything and everything."

"Where's her stronghold located? Can you show us the way?"

Flutter let out an incredulous laugh. "Seriously? Are you jesting? I'll not subject myself or my clan to that *monster* you travel with."

"He's not a monster. Xander is in servitude to the Great Wizard. So, the same protection you have for the Peacekeepers extends to him by default. You don't know him like I do, which is your loss. Why everyone sees a monster is beyond me. I know that he's an ass but there's more to him than that."

Flutter took to the air and hovered with the rest of her clan, hands firmly on her hips. "It doesn't work that way with us. If you want more information, then keep traveling this road. It will lead you to the monarchy that resides there in Herrosa. If you choose to hunt this necromancer down, just follow the stench of death and dark magic. She and her followers aren't discreet."

At once, the pixies flew off together in unison. Selandra stood there, feeling frustrated by their little welcoming party. She kneeled down and put her hand on the mossy side of the road. She opened her senses, trying to get a feel for their surroundings. The mage gasped as she easily picked up on the dark energies permeating from the environment. She felt like Flutter's assessment was correct. It felt like a sickness, infecting everything.

The mage stood back up and examined her hand. She wasn't sure why but it felt as though the dark taint was trying to seep through her skin. Xander appeared next to the Peacekeeper and said, "To the monarchy or the necromancer? Those little bugs were so informative."

Selandra looked down at her partner, who was grinning ear to ear, and stated, "I take it that you were eavesdropping on the conversation?"

The Dampire shrugged. "I was in a tree over there. I didn't trust them so I kept a watchful eye on them. I was prepared to eat again, if necessary."

"So, which way do you think?"

"I say let's go see the monarchy. We might get better information from them since they are being vexed by this dark conjurer," Xander stated. As the pair strolled down the road, the Dampire added, "They might allow us to collect the bounty on the necromancer. If so, you wouldn't have to go back to the spire."

"What bounty and why would I have to leave the spire? You know that it's forbidden for me to do so. I'd be marked for death."

"My source said that the kingdom of Herrosa is offering lordship, lands, and people to rule over as you see fit. You would be a queen."

"How come I've never heard of this," Selandra asked, confusion showed on her visage. "Who's your source?"

Xander looked up at her and said, "Andrea. The barmaid that your mage clansman immolated. She told me this so that I wouldn't kill her."

"You keep saying that I should be the one to collect this bounty." The mage glanced at him nervously, her lips almost quivering. "If we take her down, you get to have your share. Do you not want to be with me after all we've been through so far?"

Xander stopped and turned to her. He could sense her heart rate speeding up, which he stated, "I've told you before that I want you to be happy and live your life. Being tied to the Peacekeeper's ways and to me will only cause you pain and despair. I have no clue if it's the bond we share that makes you want to be with me or not, but I know for a fact that you're better off with someone else that can make life enjoyable. You deserve happiness. With me, all you'll get is suffering, heartache, and death."

"Bond or not," Selandra replied, trying to keep the tears from leaking from her eyes and staying composed, "I'd choose a short life with you over any other relationship. I know that you're trying to push me away to protect me. Just know that I can take care of myself and make my own choices."

The Dampire locked his gaze with the mage and solemnly replied, "Then prepare for a short life of pain. You got saddled with a monster against your will. One that will eventually hurt you beyond comprehension. I deserve nothing from anyone or from you for that matter. You should've let Merrick end me. It's what I richly deserve. You saw my demonic transformation; I *am* a monster."

Selandra's anger flared as she squatted down and smacked Xander's diminutive visage. The Dampire didn't flinch but he did notice that she was rubbing her palm as she snarled, "Don't you dare say that to me! I love you, damnit! I'd rather die knowing that I spent the best days of my life with you than some other cretin at the spire. Sure, we've had some intense moments thus far, but when I saw Merrick trying to decapitate you while draining the life from you, I knew, in that moment, that I didn't want to see you die."

Xander's little shoulders sagged in defeat. "You're a fool, Sel. I don't deserve you, your loyalty or your love. You can be a queen here with a better man for a king than myself."

The Peacekeeper wrapped her arms around his diminutive form. "I know that you feel that way, but I know that you heard what I said to that pixie about you. I meant every word of it. You're an ass, but I don't see the monster everyone else claims you to be, including you."

Xander's emotions were running the gambit from irritation to remorse. Why her words affected him, the Dampire couldn't say. He didn't want her to let go of his little body, but the mage did. Selandra stood up and stated, "Come on, partner. Let's go see the monarchy about a certain dark thorn in their realm."

Xander nodded and replied with amusement as they walked in tandem, "I'm sure that they'll be thrilled to see me."

"Have you been there before?"

"Not for a while," Xander answered honestly, "but my reputation may give them reason to attack or simply toss us both in a dungeon."

Chapter Twelve

They approached a small village that stood before the main stone walls of the castle. Xander noticed that there were other villages surrounding the structure off in the distance. With the threat of the necromancer, the Dampire wondered why the royal family that ruled over the realm of Herrosa chose not to erect a defensive barrier to protect their subjects.

Selandra felt the wary eyes of the unseen villagers watching them as the dirt road gave way to a cobblestone street. Doors and window shutters slammed shut as the duo walked past each structure.

"A quaint and welcoming community," Xander said sarcastically loud enough for the villagers to hear.

"Cut these people some slack," Selandra admonished. "They're being harassed by the necromancer and the undead. These people have every right to be cautious of strangers."

"Maybe," Xander mused as he watched more shutters slamming shut, catching the telling looks of disgust on each of the villagers' faces. For some reason, the Dampire had a feeling that he was the reason for their behavior and it bothered him in several ways.

One, he never got bothered by it. It came with his birthright. Two, Xander was an abomination, one that disgusted everyone, but why now did it vex him? The reputation the Dampire got during the Fae war kept many races away and for good reason.

Xander wondered if it had something to do with the bond with Selandra. It was the only logical reason that would make him feel this way.

Fucking Zerron!

Xander seethed at the thought of the Great Wizard. He created the bond between him and Selandra. *Meddling old fool! I'll gut him the moment these wardings are finally broken,* the Dampire mused to himself.

Several people saw the duo and ran ahead towards the castle. Xander sighed as if bored. "Get ready for our welcoming party, Sel."

The mage was about to reply when several horns blared from the entrance of the castle. The iron spiked gate raised up and a small band of knights rode out on their warhorses. They were all clad in shiny but scuffed up armor with chainmail underneath it. The chainmail covered most of their heads with a skull cap snuggly in place. The knights surrounded them with their weapons drawn as one of them demanded, "Halt! What business do you have here? Why do you approach?"

"We approach because we can and there's nothing that you can do about it. Now you be good little tin cans and lead us to your monarchs," Xander mocked with a toothy grin.

"Strong boasting from a tiny gnat won't get you anywhere near them!" The knight replied as he poked the Dampire's chest with the tip of his sword.

Before Xander could reply, Selandra intervened. "We're Peacekeepers of Le'orn and are here to learn more about the necromancer and put an end to her dark machinations. Will you allow us entry?"

The knight threatening Xander glanced at the mage with skepticism. "The two of you against her and her undead minions? One would think that the Great Wizard would send more Peacekeepers. Besides, we need more warriors and less mages around here. Who's to say that you won't do like all the others before you and fall to her temptations of power?"

"Isn't it obviously," Xander replied with a smirk as he ran his gray claws along the edges of the knight's sword. "To take out the necromancer, you need a monster of equal status. You people are in luck and we're here to collect the bounty on her pretty little head. I ask you this, *Asinus,* what monster do you know of that's worse than her?"

"My name is Damon and if you dare to insult me again, I'll-"

"Wait," an older knight placed a hand on Damon's shoulder, "don't do it. Not with that one. It's not worth losing your life when there are so few of us to protect the realm."

"Are you questioning my authority, Garrett?"

"No, my dear Captain," Garrett solemnly replied as his graying eyes fell on the Dampire, "I'm advising you to use caution, especially when you are addressing the Abominable Butcher. That's who you are, unless my eyes deceive me."

Damon scoffed, "Am I to be afraid of something so small? I could easily trample him with my horse."

Garrett roughly squeezed the captain's shoulder, causing the armor to creak. "You weren't a part of the Fae war like I was. I'll never forget his face or his name."

"You expect me to let this fiend into the castle to talk with the royal family? He can't be trusted and you know it."

"Good point, but I know for a fact that if he gives his word, rest assured that he will abide by it. You don't go making deals with this devil lightly," Garrett spoke with a hint of anxiety.

Xander smiled and said, "What your man there says is true. I give my word that I will be cordial within your walls, but be warned. If anyone attempts any form of bodily harm against Selandra or myself, then consider this agreement broken and then you will discover why I'm known as the Abominable Butcher."

As all eyes fell on the Captain, Garrett dismounted from his warhorse and walked towards the Dampire. He dropped down to one knee and got eye to eye with Xander and said with a nervous smile, "It is you, Xander Bane. My apologies for not recognizing you. My eyesight isn't what it was during the war. How are you, my old friend?"

Selandra looked on as not only the other knights murmured amongst themselves, but so did the more braver peasants. She wondered if they knew his name better than the mocking moniker the vampires gave him. More weapons were drawn by the onlookers as soon as the knight said Xander's name so she announced, "Does Xander Bane need to set an example for those who wish us harm?"

The knights looked at the mage with confusion, but Damon understood as he snapped his head in the direction of the growing mob. The captain barked out, "Stand down, everyone!"

"That's Xander Bane," one woman cried out in disgust. "The beast needs to be put down!"

The Dampire looked at Garrett, unfazed by the peasant's threat, "As you can see, young man, I'm loved no matter where I go. What can I say? I'm popular. What say you, Garrett? Do you wish to see the dance of death on these people or on display against the necromancer and her army?"

The elder knight looked up at Damon and said with panic laced in his stern voice, "Captain, I can vouch for Xander. His word is his bond and he always follows through. He will slaughter the villagers faster than the blink of an eye. Trust me, accept his terms."

Damon curtly nodded and motioned to the other knights. "Right. Escort these two to the royal court. Garrett, disperse the villagers."

As the knights led them into the castle, cries rang out from the angry mob. Xander smirked as he crossed the threshold of the main entrance. Selandra looked back at the crowd and saw that they were fleeing. Reanimated corpses moved amongst them, grabbing and biting any that were too slow.

Damon ordered the other knights as he saw Garrett hacking at the dead, "Clear the streets of the dead, now!"

"Trouble in paradise, Damon?" Xander asked with a grin.

"If you're as great as Garrett says that you are, why don't you help out?" the captain growled.

"Because we're here to see the monarchy about it. We're not doing anything for you for free. I may be in the service of the Great Wizard Zerron but that doesn't make me obligated to assist you in this trivial crisis."

As more peasants cried out in terror, the captain looked to the mage for help. Selandra pressed the Dampire, "Xander, we should help these people."

"Give me a reason, Sel," Xander retorted.

"If we collect the bounty on the necromancer and there's no peasants left, who would we rule over? Don't you hear them calling for aid?"

"I do," the Dampire replied as he pointed at them, "and I also recall them wanting to kill me. Fitting end to the mob, if you ask me."

"Xander-"

"Fine," the Dampire curtly cut her off, "I'll deal with these gnats. Head to the royal court and I'll be along shortly, my dear."

Xander smacked the Peacekeeper on her ass and then stated to Damon, "Care to see what your kingdom is buying?"

The captain motioned to several servants. "You two! Escort the Peacekeeper to the royal court. I'm coming with you, Xander. I want to see if you're really as good as Garrett claims."

"Try and keep up, tin man," Xander exclaimed as he teleported away. Selandra walked away with her new escorts as Damon ordered, "All that needs sanctuary, head to the castle!"

As peasants rushed past the captain, he watched as the Dampire appeared all over the place. He was cutting the reanimated corpses down swiftly with his magical blade. As Damon reached Garrett, he put his back against his and said, "You didn't mention that he wielded such a strange weapon."

"He didn't have it in the war. That's a new addition," the elder knight replied as he hacked and slashed at several reanimated corpses encroaching on him. "He's deadly unarmed. Now, Xander appears to be unstoppable."

More guards rushed out of the castle as Damon watched the Dampire appear on top of a roof. Xander looked at him and smiled as he shouted, "Enjoying the demonstration?"

Xander teleported down in front of a cowering woman next to a wagon trailer and cut down three of the undead. He looked up at her and was about to say something when she spat on his face. "Get away from me, *monster*!"

"That's gratitude for you," the Dampire said as he wiped the spittle off. "Run along before you get yourself into more trouble."

The woman cried out angrily as she swiped and thrust her sword at the diminutive Dampire. Xander dodged each blow with ease before teleporting onto her back. He bit down viciously into the peasant's neck, causing her to scream. The woman attempted to slash at Xander with her sword, but ended up dropping it in mid swing.

The peasant crumbled down to her knees, moaning and sobbing. Xander yanked his fangs from her neck and coldly whispered into her ear, "You wanted me, well now you have me. Don't worry, wench! You won't die from my teeth. Enjoy your undead friends and thanks for the meal."

The woman's eyes fluttered as her body sagged against a wagon wheel as the Dampire teleported away. The peasant barely registered the reanimated corpses encroaching on her until the biting began. Xander reappeared next to the Captain and Garrett with blood smeared over his mouth. Damon glared at the Dampire as he licked his lips

"Why did you kill that woman, you fiend!"

"I saved her and then she got what she deserved for crossing me. I'm sure that the undead will find her flesh delectable," Xander replied, not caring at all as the captain berated him.

"All these villagers are important to the well-being of Herrosa. They're our citizens and we've sworn to protect them!"

"I never gave that oath, so I'm exempt to do what I please. Now, if you don't mind, I have a meeting to attend."

"Help us, Xander," Garrett pleaded as he severed another head. "I'm sure that there's some kind of compensation you will take to help."

"That's why I'm meeting your ruling family." Xander grinned and, before he teleported away, he added, "Find where they're coming from and kill the summoner."

The Dampire focused on Selandra by using the bond that they unwillingly shared together and appeared in front of her, startling the servants. He chuckled as he walked beside Selandra. "You people act as though you've seen a ghost."

"Behave, Xander," the mage chided. "Everyone here is on edge. Now, did you deal with the dead outside?

"For the most part, yes," Xander replied as he clasped his hands behind his back. "I'm confident that the guards can clean up the remnants that are still lingering about."

Selandra groaned mentally as they rounded the corner that led down a long corridor. There was a thick purple running rug that led all the way to a pair of ornate oak double doors where four guards stood as sentinels on either side. Along the walls was floor to ceiling pane glass windows, the light of the sun that came through created a myriad of colors that twinkled on the floor.

One of the double doors opened abruptly and a tall figure stepped out. As the door closed behind him, Selandra could tell that he was Fae. He had pale, unblemished skin with long flowing hair that cascaded down his back. The points of his ears poked out prominently. He was dressed in bright yellow and orange garments accented by his weaponry.

He squinted at the Dampire and then a brief look of recognition crossed the fae warrior's visage. He towered over Xander for a moment and then, he surprised Selandra by dropping down to one knee.

"Master Bane," the fae warrior spoke in a monotonous voice as he put his hand on the Dampire's little shoulder. "It's good to see you, my old friend."

"Fal'destion, I see that you still live, old man. What brings you here?"

The Peacekeeper could sense a change in Xander's attitude and demeanor as he interacted with the fae warrior. It was obvious to her that they had a history, but there didn't seem to be any kind of animosity.

Were they friends?

A slight curl of Fal'destion's lips was the most emotion he showed. "I could ask you the same question, but I have a feeling that it has to do with the troubles occurring here."

"Astute, as always. We're here to take on the supposed bounty on the necromancer."

Fal curtly nodded and then asked as he examined the Dampire closely, "You're different. You have some nasty wardings on your person." He glanced up at the Peacekeeper as he added, "Are you this one's prisoner?"

A snort escaped Selandra before she could suppress it, causing the pair to look at her. "Hardly. I'm not *that* skilled. I'm his handler and an extension of the Great Wizard Zerron of Le'orn."

"Selandra gets all modest when it comes to her skill sets. Don't let her fool you. She bested me in combat and put me in my current situation with the Peacekeepers."

Fal'destion had a look of surprise for a moment before looking at the Peacekeeper. Selandra felt his piercing gaze assessing her, which made her want to hide herself in her cloak. The Fae warrior cocked his head and said, "I can see an unusual bond between you two. Might I inquire about it?"

Xander looked up at the mage. He could feel her heart rate increasing, her breathing was coming in short bursts. The Dampire smiled. "Sel doesn't have a choice in the matter. Zerron bound us together as a way to keep me on a short leash. She's a highly skilled and an intelligent woman that deserves a better job than being stuck with me. I'm sure you can understand why?"

Fal'destion curtly nodded as he stood back up. He turned to Selandra and said,

"How do you truly feel about him? Humor me, if you will."

Selandra blushed as the fae warrior focused his full attention on her. She did her best to shift the conversation back to him. "You never answered Xander's query. Why are you here?"

"A great pairing," Fal'destion stated with a slight smirk. "I'm here as an emissary for my people. I had the task to assess the situation here."

"Does that mean that the Fae are going to intervene," Xander asked.

"If it were up to me," Fal stated as he tore his eyes from the mage to the Dampire, "I'd have several raiding parties here to rid the area of the necromancer and her taint on the land."

"I'm sensing a but coming," Selandra said, feeling like she could tell that this warrior was ready to go take out the necromancer.

"The ruling Fae don't see why they should intervene. The realm of Herrosa allowed her to come into power and it's believed that they should deal with her. The bounty is a good idea, but the Fae aren't tempted by it. I have a different task that I must attend to in another realm. One that makes the dark conjurer of these lands look like a novice."

Xander nodded with concern etched in his face. "Do they know about her alliance with the vampires?"

"If they know, then I'm not privy to it. You know me, Xander, and I, you. If you're here to deal with her then I know that she's as good as dead, like her army. If you don't veer from the task, that is," Fal said with a knowing look.

"Whatever do you mean by that," the Dampire asked, feigning surprise. He grinned, revealing his fangs. "I always stick to a plan. Without question."

Fal'destion raised an eyebrow and nodded to the mage and Xander before marching off. Selandra watched him leave and then asked, "What was he referring to, Xander?"

"Another story for another time. Ask me again later, love," the Dampire replied as he pointed to the double doors. "I believe that we're going to find out if we will be granted an audience."

Chapter Thirteen

A gangly man walked towards them. His face was gaunt to the point of being skeletal and covered in age spots and wrinkles. Despite the man's outward appearance, Selandra couldn't help but wonder if this was natural aging or related to the troubles here because the man moved like he had the vitality of a twenty-year-old.

It was obvious that the man disliked the Dampire as he sneered when his eyes fell on him. The servants stepped forward as the gangly man barked, "Who are these two and why have you allowed this filth into the castle?"

"These two seek an audience with the royal family, Reed," one of the servants spoke up with fear laced in his voice.

"We're from Le'orn," the mage announced as she stepped forward. "My name is Selandra and this is-"

"I know who and what that *thing* is!" Reed snapped, cutting the mage off. He pointed at Xander and snarled, "He's not welcome here. Leave now or-"

"Or what?" Xander hissed, tiring of being berated. He teleported on Reed's back, causing the guards at the doors to rush forward. The Dampire whispered in his ear, "We're here to save your pathetic asses from the necromancer. Should I add you to my list? You look like one of her undead minions. Be a sport and let us in, *now!*"

Reed looked at Selandra, his eyes pleading for her to help. The mage smirked as Xander licked the man's neck and she commented, "I think an apology is in order."

Reed nervously bit out, "A what? Why?"

Selandra looked at the Dampire and said, "For your blatant disrespectful attitude towards Xander and myself. Your station may grant you certain privileges, but they don't shield you from his bite."

Reed yelped when he felt the Dampire's fangs graze his skin, drawing blood. He licked the wound and said, "Your blood ensures that

I can find you no matter where you go. Drop the attitude, do your job, and usher us in."

The guards pointed their swords at the Dampire as Reed audibly gulped. He glanced at Xander and said, "My apologies. If you'll get off me, I'll take you both inside."

Xander kissed him on the cheek, causing Reed to grimace in disgust, and then he teleported himself next to the mage. The Dampire adjusted his jacket as Reed waved off the guards. "It's all right. Just a simple misunderstanding. Back to your posts men."

The guards sheathed their swords but surrounded them as the gangly man led the way to the double doors. Selandra glared at Xander and said under her breath, "Your antics are going to get us both killed."

"You're probably right," Xander replied, but in no way did he feel any shame, "which will make every mission that we have together much more interesting."

"I guess that my life is truly forfeit," the mage replied bitterly. "I can see it now: You will create a bit of trouble and my head will be mounted on a spike somewhere."

As they crossed the threshold into the royal court, the Dampire remarked, "And this is exactly why I believe that you deserve someone better to be with than myself, Sel."

The royal court room was circular in design, rows of wooden benches lined the room. Towards the front were two thrones crafted from gold with the royal crest carved at the top and upholstered with thick, purple padding. A large oak table sat in front where both the king and queen, as well as their advisory council, intently scrutinized over a map of the realm.

As a heated discussion escalated, Reed nervously announced, "Representatives of Le'orn wish for an audience."

At the mention of Le'orn, everyone stopped talking. When all eyes fell on them, half the council blanched seeing the Dampire. Xander smirked as he crossed his arms behind his back and said, "We hear that your realm is being harried by a dark sorcerer. Is the bounty on her pretty little head still available or was that just a rumor?"

No one spoke. They weren't sure what to make of the Dampire and feared that he might slaughter them all outright. Xander nudged Selandra, ushering her forward to address the royal court.

"The Peacekeepers of Le'orn have heard of this necromancer and would like to offer our services to rid your realm of her. Both Xander and I have already encountered some of her minions and-"

"How is it that the Abominable Butcher is considered a part of the Peacekeepers," one of the advisors blurted out, interrupting the mage with a sneer.

Before the Dampire could reply, the king reprimanded, "Now that's no way to welcome our allies. If the Dampire is working for the Great Wizard, so be it." His eyes fell on Xander as he added, "My most sincere apologies, Master Bane. Please forgive Beck. He, like all of us I'm sure, is feeling overwhelmed by our current plight."

"I must say that I'm intrigued by your presence, Master Bane," the queen spoke, sounding polished and poised. "If you're here to aid us against the necromancer, then we should be grateful for it. Don't you agree, Beck?"

"But, my queen," Beck stammered as he pointed his finger at Xander. "He's not any better than that necromancer. Are we truly going to consider being bedfellows with this *monster*?"

"If you have something to say, Beck," the Dampire replied, not caring about protocol, "then say what's on your mind."

"Yes. We are no better than the necromancer if we were to align with *you*."

"I can vouch for Xander," Selandra stated as her anger came to the forefront. Her hands were clenched as she hid them in her cloak. "He's in servitude of the Great Wizard Zerron as punishment for his willful breaking of the Vampire Pact. Do you want Le'orn to support you or do wish to let fear rule over you?"

The queen, along with the others in the room, looked at Beck. He backed away and bit out, "Sire, you can't be seriously considering that we trade one monster for another?"

"A monster I am," Xander replied coldly, "but sometimes, you need a monster to do what needs to be done."

Selandra glanced down at the Dampire. She could tell that he believed this and it upset her. *Why does everyone have to see the monster first? Why not give him a chance to prove his worth?*

"Master Bane, Beck does not speak for all of us. Herrosa would be indebted to you and the Peacekeepers of Le'orn, if you were to stop the necromancer once and for all. To answer your question, yes, the bounty is still available. A kingdom of your own with people who you can rule over as you see fit and the spoils that come with it. My name is Duncan and this is my lovely queen Ramona. We know of your namesake and your reputation as a bounty hunter, but whom is this that travels with you?"

The Peacekeeper proudly stepped forward. "My name is Selandra. I'm Master Bane's handler and an extension of the Great Wizard Zerron. He wants to know more about the necromancer and frankly, so do we. What can you tell us about her?"

"This is utter madness," Beck spat out. "If he collects the bounty, then we're all as good as dead. I'm sorry your majesty, but I can't be a part of this. I have to argue against using this *beast* before us."

"What exactly has Xander done to warrant such hatred? Is this about the war or did he actually do something to you?" Selandra asked, the ire for the advisor showing.

"His existence is enough reason to dismiss him from the realm. If it were up to me-"

"Thankfully," King Duncan cut Beck off, "the decision isn't up to you. The last time I checked, I *do* have the final say. Can you truly stand there and choose to squander an opportunity like this as the dead encroach upon our kingdom?"

Gasps escaped from both the royal family and the advisors as Xander teleported himself on to the top of the table. He examined the map, disappointed that it wasn't a world map of Dragermora, and said, "Point us in her direction and we'll clear her out. If not," the Dampire eyed Beck and added coldly, "I'm sure that we'll return as one of the dead and eat everyone in sight."

Beck gulped as he tore his eyes away from Xander. King Duncan pointed at a small mark that resembled a skull on the map and said, "The best we can tell is that she's here. It's difficult to get proper intel when most don't return. Alive, that is. The other marks are areas that the undead have attacked."

"What else can we expect to encounter," Selandra asked as she stepped up to the table. She saw the skull mark but it didn't feel right to her. Her instincts were forcing her eyes to the west of the mark, to a small mountainous range.

"Normally, there's the usual predators like the panthers and wolves, but I'm not sure if they're around anymore," Damon answered as he entered the room along with Garrett. Both knights were panting as they kneeled down, their armor was now dented and covered in gore. "Hunting parties tend to run into the dead so it's hard to say if the natural predators moved out of the area or died."

The Dampire squatted down next to the Peacekeeper and asked, "You sensing something, Sel?"

"Yes." Selandra pointed at the mountains. "What's in this region here?"

"That area is known as Capricorn Range," King Duncan answered. He motioned for the knights to come forward. "It's been quiet lately. Our usual threat that resides there hasn't been seen in months."

"What threat is that?" Xander asked as he stroked his chin.

"The goatmen." Damon spat as he said the name. "Foul creatures. They live in the mountains and raid the surrounding settlements for food and women for breeding purposes."

"There's more there than just the goatmen," Garrett added as he pointed to the base of the mountain range. "Leapers swarm around the foothills and in the trees, killing indiscriminately for their next meal. They see you; they attack. Best keep your wits about you and your eyes on the canopy."

The queen looked at the mage and asked, "How many Peacekeepers will the Great Wizard Zerron be sending with you?"

Xander smirked as he hopped off the table, landing quietly next to Selandra. "I'm fairly certain that you're looking at the extent of his forces for this little trek."

Gasps and arguing ensued amongst the royal court. Selandra could see a myriad of emotions crossing their countenances, except for Beck. He malevolently grinned at Xander, as if this revelation amused him. King Duncan raised his hand and said, "Enough. I understand that the Great Wizard can't send an army of mages, but why send just the two of you alone? Can you explain the rationale for this choice?"

Selandra looked down at the Dampire, looking to him for an answer. She wasn't fully sure why Zerron didn't want to give her and Xander proper backup. The Dampire turned his attention to the monarchy and said, "Why send a battalion when he has me instead? Zerron is preparing for war and we're gathering intel and eliminating threats."

"Who has declared war on the Peacekeepers of Le'orn?" Queen Ramona asked.

Selandra confidently replied, "Your little necromancer has. She has created an alliance with the vampires. Who's to say that she hasn't enlisted the goatmen of the Capricorn Range? Many are flocking to her darkness and the promise of power."

"I'm certain that she's planning on waging war on the Fae and any that stand with them," Xander proclaimed as he slowly paced back and forth. "The way I see it, the

Peacekeepers of Le'orn are a target since they enforce pacts and treaties that favor the victors of the war. It's very well that she has spies listening in to conversations all over this region, so Herrosa is on the list. Having an audience with the Fae would be enough to deem you an enemy, but then again, you're already fighting her. I'm sure that you can think of other races that would love an opportunity to take out the ruling Fae."

"What about you, Xander?" Beck sneered, his disgust obvious. "Where do you fit in? Which side are you on, *Butcher*?"

"I'm on my own side because no one else can convince me that it's the wrong one," Xander answered as his gaze fell on Selandra. He could tell that she didn't like what he said, so he added, "But unlike the last war, I won't be going to battle alone. Of all the Peacekeepers of Le'orn, I got lucky to get the brightest and most talented mage of them all and I wouldn't have it any other way. That said, do we have an accord for the bounty, your majesty?"

Selandra smiled as her cheeks reddened. The king thought for a moment and then countered, "I have a few stipulations. There's a man that has been inquiring about the bounty. If you would take him with you, I'd feel better about your chances of success. I was hoping to have him go with the Fae, but since they have declined, I was about to dismiss him. One man against the sheer numbers that the necromancer has at her disposal would mean certain death."

"Where is this man at?" Selandra asked.

King Duncan motioned to one of the guards and said, "He's waiting in the study for my decision. I said that he's a fool for wanting to take on the task alone, but he was insistent. He claims that it's the only way to clear up a huge debt."

Xander chuckled to himself as the doors opened. Reed came in first, nervously eyeing the Dampire, and trailing behind him was Orimus. The assassin's eyes fell on Xander as he pointed his finger and snarled, "What the hell is that *abomination* doing here? You're here to steal yet another bounty from me, aren't you? Say the word, your highness, and I'll gladly end this creature's existence!"

Chapter Fourteen

"Friend of yours, Xander?" Selandra muttered as she grabbed her staff and pointed it at Orimus.

"He's the one that's been making my coin pouch jingle with more gold. Meet Orimus. Former leader of the Assassin's Guild and disgraced bounty hunter. Desperate times make for awkward alliances, don't they? How's your neck by the way?" The Dampire grinned at the assassin.

As the assassin rushed forward, both Damon and Garrett unsheathed their swords. Orimus stopped as the tips of the blades were inches from his chest and demanded, "Peacekeeper! Do you not know who stands beside you? He's the-"

"He has a name and it's Xander Bane. I know of his crimes and he's serving his sentence as we speak. I'm sure that you realize that you've incriminated yourself as one of the assassins that fled the guild. I should immolate you on general principle."

The assassin blanched as Xander cackled. Orimus looked at the monarchy and said, "Why are they here? I thought you wanted me to go with the Fae."

King Duncan replied, "The Fae refused to intercede with our problem. The Peacekeepers are here to put an end to the necromancer, so if you want to have a chance to clear up your monetary debt, I suggest that you go with them."

"You can't be serious?" Orimus bit out, feeling stunned. "I can do this task better on my own."

"I suggest that you listen to the king," Garrett stated. He glanced down at the Dampire and added, "With Xander, at least you have a fighting chance. His companion must be a formidable warrior to be able to keep up with the Dampire. You should heed the king's decision because it's not a request."

The assassin's shoulders slumped as his voice deflated with resignation. "This can't be happening. It's the guild all over again."

Xander teleported beside Orimus and smacked him on his ass and said cheerfully, "Cheer up, weepy, and look on the bright side, you get the pleasure of my company once again. Just like old times."

"Garrett," the queen spoke with a calm but commanding cadence, "will you guide them to the Capricorn Range?"

"If it means the end of the necromancer's reign of terror, then yes." The elder knight dropped down to one knee. "I shall serve the realm of Herrosa until my last breath."

Xander rolled his eyes. "We don't have time for formalities. You can guide us there, but when we're in sight of the mountain range, you can turn back. Herrosa will need you here once we kick the proverbial hornet's nest."

"Do you not think that I can fight?" Garrett looked up at the Dampire with fire in his aging eyes.

"On the contrary, my old friend," Xander replied. He placed his little hand on the knight's shoulder. "Never assume that I think that of you. You asked me earlier what my price was for help, well here it is. Guide us there and I'll see to it that you return without incident. I mean it when I say your skills are needed here. You have my word, Garrett."

The elder knight sheepishly smiled. "Teleportation. I suppose that it's a good thing I ate a light breakfast."

Xander chuckled as the elder knight stood up. He looked to the monarchs and said, "I'll get our provisions ready and meet them at the gate." Garrett nodded at the captain as he turned on his heels and marched out of the court yard.

"Damon," the king ordered, "have all available guards and knights ready for a siege. They might slay the necromancer but that won't stop her allies from retaliating."

"As you command, my liege," the captain of the knights replied with his hand over his heart and a slight bow. As Damon left, Xander looked over at Beck and asked, "Can we take Beck with us too?"

Beck nervously looked between the Dampire and the rest of the royal court. The queen answered with curiosity. "Beck isn't a warrior. He's an advisor that's never seen combat. Why would you want him?"

"I get famished easily and I figure Beck could keep my hunger at bay," Xander replied as he flashed his fangs at Beck. The advisor paled as he fled the room in a panic, screaming incoherently. The Dampire looked back at the monarchs and asked, "Did I say something wrong?"

"Everything about you is wrong, *abomination*," Orimus sneered. As he stormed out, he added, "I'm going to wait at the gate and assist the knight."

Queen Ramona assessed the Peacekeeper and said, "You look famished, my dear. It will take some time to prepare the provisions, will you join us for dinner?"

"Gladly, your majesty," Selandra said and then looked at Xander, "but only if my partner can join us as well."

King Duncan had a look of surprise. "You can eat food, Master Bane?"

"Everyone seems so surprised by this little fact," Xander replied with a smile. "I'm part demon after all. It's why I managed to survive under the terms of the Vampire Pact."

Selandra rolled her eyes as the king clapped his hands twice. "Reed, escort our guests to the great hall."

"Yes, my liege." Reed rushed in and motioned to the Dampire and Peacekeeper. "Follow me this way."

Reed led them out of the courtyard, winding their way through the various corridors. Each one had long purple tapestries hanging on them with the royal crest, sconces made of pure gold lit the way. Selandra wondered if they would make it to the great hall before starvation kicked in. Her stomach growled, which caused Xander to glance at her.

"You should've had a snack, like I did earlier, and then your belly wouldn't be complaining."

"I don't want to think about the *snack* you ate. He had a name," Selandra replied with a sour look on her face.

"And now he's swimming in my stomach. That pixie got what he rightfully deserved for threatening us," Xander said with a shrug.

Reed turned down another long corridor and marched over to a maroon door. He pulled on the handle and motioned for them to enter. The great hall had six rows of long tables, running the length of the room. Another long table sat at the end on a raised portion of the stone floor for the monarchy and esteemed guests.

More tapestries hung from the walls on gold rods. Servants and wait staff bustled about, frantically setting up the feast. Floral decorations and candelabras sat in the center of each table. Selandra's mouth salivated as the food came out on multiple dinner carts. King Duncan and his queen entered through a side door and took their place in the middle of the elevated table. The king motioned at them as he said, "Come and join us. Others will be along shortly."

Xander walked over to the monarchy table with the mage beside him. He pulled out a chair for Selandra. She warmly smiled at the Dampire as he slid her chair towards the table. Xander didn't bother pulling a chair out for himself. The Dampire teleported on the seat and patiently waited to be served.

More people trickled into the room, mostly peasants as far as Xander could tell, followed by the knights and Orimus. Xander eyed the assassin as he smirked, garnering a glare from his former guild leader. As the plates were filled, Selandra ate several grapes from a fruit platter in front of them.

Orimus chose to sit with the knights, not wanting to be near the Dampire. The feast consisted of wild boar, rabbit, deer along with various fruits and vegetables platters. Selandra wasn't sure what to make of the spread but her stomach demanded that she partake in the abundant meal.

Servants walked by, pouring wine and tending to everyone as the guests talked amongst themselves. The Peacekeeper looked down at her plate and saw that it was filled with hot steaming food. Perplexed, she glanced at Xander, who shrugged and said, "Eat up, Sel. You'll need your strength so fill that little belly of yours, my dear."

King Duncan raised his goblet and tapped on it repeatedly with his spoon. The room went quiet as the king stood up and spoke. "I wish that we were dining under better circumstances, but I fear that darker days are still ahead. The blight on our realm not only vexes us, but I understand that the dark conjurer is spreading her taint to other realms. Many have tried to rid us of the necromancer and her dark forces and have failed. But, as fate would have it, we've been blessed with the presence of the Peacekeepers of Le'orn." He motioned over at Selandra and Xander. "They've graciously come to us of their own accord to go and deal with our enemies on our behalf. For this, I raise my goblet to you and pray that Dracon watches over you."

Many cheers ensued, which made Selandra want to shy away. *No pressure,* the mage thought to herself. She felt a small hand squeeze her thigh and then heard the Dampire speak to her in her head. "*Might be a daunting task for us, but we can handle this necromancer. Now smile and enjoy yourself, Queen Selandra.*"

The mage warmly smiled at the king as she mentally replied, "*You're getting ahead of yourself, don't you think? We were barely able to deal with the undead and Merrick. What makes you so confident that we have a chance against the necromancer?*"

Xander stuffed a fork full of meat into his mouth and smiled at her. "*Together, we're unstoppable. I'm not saying that we won't get our hair mussed. In the end, she will fall. If not, war will break out once more.*"

"Like I said," Selandra muttered, "no pressure."

Xander surveyed the great hall and noticed that many of the people were looking at him. His acute hearing allowed him to hear snippets of each conversation, which seemed to revolve around him. Xander flashed his fangs, causing many onlookers to flinch, before stuffing more meat into his deadly maw.

Selandra bumped him with her elbow and whispered, "Stop playing with the food and eat your food. I don't want you to make a spectacle."

"It's not my problem. They keep discussing if I'm the Abominable Butcher so I showed them." Xander looked up at the mage curiously. "Why did you refer to those people as food?"

"Technically, they're food to you. It's not like I can stop you from drinking the entire room dry. So, I must insist that you behave."

"As you wish, your highness." Xander chuckled, eyeing the scowling mage over the rim of his goblet as he drank. One of the peasants stood up and asked, "How many

Peacekeepers will be coming? I see only the female. Are there more on the way?"

King Duncan looked over at Selandra and said, "What you see before you is who we have at this time. I believe that the Peacekeepers of Le'orn don't need to show up all at once. I shall defer to Selandra here to answer your question since she knows more about it than I do."

The mage stood up slowly, leaving her hood up for effect as she made her eyes glow. "The Peacekeepers of Le'orn can portal in at any time, anywhere. Xander Bane and myself are here to-"

"The Abominable Butcher!" An older woman cried out. "You bring that *beast* into our realm? Why would you do this?"

"Simple," the Dampire replied as he teleported himself next to the woman, startling her. "I'm the best bounty hunter around and I plan on collecting the bounty on the necromancer. When that happens, you can refer to me as King Abominable Butcher."

Xander lifted his goblet and cheerfully exclaimed, "Fresh blood for life!"

"You can't be serious?" another peasant blurted out. "I don't want that *thing* near my family, let alone ruling over the realm!"

Xander's gaze fell on the man as he coldly spoke. "Then, by all means, go slay the necromancer and claim it for yourself. I won't stop you. I'll sit back and watch you fight your way through the dead. I'm sure that you must be a formidable warrior with a pitchfork and a torch."

The man backed down and cast his eyes to his semi full plate. Queen Ramona stood up and spoke with an air of confidence and authority. "Master Bane works for the Peacekeepers and has the right to claim the bounty, just like the rest of you. They'll be leaving us shortly so if anyone wishes to join their party, do so now. I don't want to hear another cross word about Xander Bane or his companion. These are dark times and we need all the aid we can get."

Selandra shook her head as she sat back down. The Dampire reappeared in his chair next to her, smiling innocently at her as he sipped from his goblet. "I tried to behave. I really did."

"Yes, it lasted for less than five minutes," Selandra replied sarcastically.

"They're alive, aren't they?" Xander spoke up loudly so others could hear him. "See? Your favorite monster can control his primal urge to rip throats out. Though I'll have no guilt in doing it if they keep it up."

A side door opened and a mountain of a man walked in the great hall. He was a burly man that was clad in a thick leather hide jacket and a blue tunic and black pants. His footfall was heavy, like his calf high boots, and it echoed in the great hall despite the crowd noise. He had a scraggly black beard with patches of silver in it, which matched his unkempt hair. The burly man kneeled down and stated, "Your highness, all the provisions are ready and waiting for the Peacekeepers and the assassin."

"Good to hear, Karl," King Duncan replied. He looked at Selandra and the Dampire and said, "If you wish to leave now, you can, but if you need rest, we can provide suitable lodging."

Orimus stood up and sneered at Xander. "If you two cretins choose to stay, I'll go ahead and deal with the necromancer. I've no need for rest. I can handle a simple sorceress!"

Selandra glared at the assassin as he marched out of the great hall. Xander tsked. "Orimus. Ever the melodramatic fool. I'd say that once you get to know him that he's different, but I'd be lying through my fangs."

"I'm surprised that he's still alive," the mage fumed. "Explain to me how you kept from killing him outright?"

"Orimus is fun to torment and he always comes back for more. What can I say, I was bored and he was a toy that I never grew tired of playing with? So, what's your choice, Sel? Stay and rest or go now?"

Selandra stood up, warmly smiling at the Dampire. "It might be wise to leave now. Who knows what kind of mess your old friend will leave in his wake? Besides," she leaned down, removed her hood, and kissed Xander on his lips, causing a stir from the onlookers, and murmured, "we both know that if we stay, neither of us will get any sleep."

"You say that like it's a bad thing, love," Xander replied as his small hand slipped between her thighs, stroking her core. "I'm ready to leave, but I'm more concerned for you. You've had a rough go thus far. Are you sure you're up for the mission?"

Xander grinned as he felt the mage lean into his hand. Her heart was racing with excitement and her cheeks were flushing. With her eyes closed, Selandra bit out, "Let's go deal with the necromancer and then," she grabbed his hand and firmly held it against her core, "you can have this once we've completed the task at hand. Deal?"

Xander groaned softly as he slid her hand down to his crotch. "I accept your terms, but know that I have no problem taking you during this *hard* trek. Garrett," he called out, "head to the gate. We have a necromancer to slay."

Xander grabbed Selandra by her hand and teleported them both away.

Chapter Fifteen

Orimus and Garrett walked out into the courtyard and saw that Xander and the Peacekeeper were waiting patiently by the loaded down horses. He sneered as the Dampire smirked. "Oh you think that you're quite clever?"

As Selandra mounted her horse, Xander merrily retorted, "If compared to you, a second-rate assassin, there's no contest. Don't come crying to me if you get yourself into trouble. I won't save your hide again."

"*Abomination*," the assassin growled as he mounted his steed. "Before this little quest is over, you will understand the meaning of pain and suffering for mocking me!"

"This is true. I know because your incessant whining is torturous on my ears," Xander countered as he teleported himself on the horse. He nestled his body against Selandra. She smiled as she adjusted the reins, embracing the Dampire with her arms.

As Garrett ordered the gate to be opened, Orimus snidely commented, "I see that the stables didn't have any miniature ponies for the *abomination*. I'm surprised that you can actually fit on a fully grown beast."

The mage glared and was ready to retort, but the Dampire beat her to it. "You should know by now that I'm full of surprises. You can call me whatever you wish, but if you refer to Selandra as a beast again, I'll enjoy watching her immolate you into a smoldering pile of ash. Trust me, I've witnessed it happen to the last person who pissed her off."

The Peacekeeper's eyes flared brightly with magic, causing the assassin to stammer, "I- I wasn't- that's not what- I would never disrespect a lady of her status. I was referring to-"

"Save it, Orimus," Selandra coldly threatened as she reached over her shoulder and touched her staff, causing the crystal to spark. "We're here to complete a mission. If need be, some dead weight can be trimmed from the party. Don't forget, I know how to find you!"

Orimus cast his eyes forward and muttered as his face reddened, "Right. I'll go ride ahead with the knight."

The mage lowered her arm as the assassin urged his steed forward. She felt a little hand grasp her other hand. Selandra looked down at the Dampire and was puzzled by the look of concern etched on his regal visage.

"Are you feeling well, Sel?" Xander asked under his breath.

"I'm fine," the mage replied, irritation laced in her voice. "What's it to you, Dampire?"

"I've noticed a subtle change in your attitude. Some of the comments you've made since we arrived here have me concerned."

"What are you referring to? I'm just-"

Xander placed the tips of his fingers on her soft lips. "I think that the dark magic that's infecting this realm is affecting you as well. Since when have you referred to people as 'food'? And just now, with that buffoon, you were fixing to burn him alive."

"Maybe I'm just tired and feeling a bit stretched," Selandra answered mentally with a slight smirk. *"We've been going on a lot of missions lately and I'm not sure how much longer I can hold out. I think that I need more downtime. We both do."*

"Sel, I can't disagree with your assessment. After we wipe the realm with the necromancer, I vow to take you wherever you wish to go in the world," Xander replied mentally as he caressed her cheeks.

"But what about Zerron and the spire-"

"Fuck him and everything and everyone at Le'orn," Xander hissed. He turned around so he was facing the mage with his arms across his chest, his eyes turning crimson. "If I could break these wardings on me, I'd gladly kill them all so you could have a chance at happiness for once in your sheltered life! I'd slaughter any that tries to prevent you from having the life you deserve."

"Xander?" Selandra gulped. "Xander, now you're scaring me. What's gotten into you?"

The Dampire cocked an eyebrow, his face was devoid of all emotions and cold. "I'm the monster that you need to fear. You should be with another, one who can grant your heart's desires. My life is full of death and I have a past that I wear like an unyielding armor that can never come off, despite what you think of me."

Selandra noticed that his demonic size was showing. Xander grew bigger and bulkier, his clothing stretched with his growth but remained intact despite the physical changes. Peasants that walked by stared and gaped at the Dampire, while others scurried away in fear. The Peacekeeper reached out for Xander and grasped his clawed hand.

She gasped as she felt so much darkness and negativity within the Dampire. Selandra wasn't sure if it was from his demonic side or not. The mage used her senses and was stunned by what she saw. Dark energy was leeching not only into Xander, but everyone, including herself. Even the land and all the plant life were permeated with it, like a terrible sickness, but Xander seemed to absorb it quicker than anything else.

Xander seemed to be affected as they traveled down a dirt trail into the forest. His eyes wavered from crimson to black, and then back to normal. Selandra halted her horse and dismounted. Xander hopped down beside her without making a sound.

"What's that *abomination* doing?" Orimus spat out. Selandra could see the fear behind the assassin's eyes.

Garrett recognized Xander morphing and said, "Dracon, help us all if he goes full on demonic."

"I-" Orimus stammered at the sight. "I never knew that he could do that. What happens if he loses control?"

"If that happens, then there's nothing we can do. We'll be dead before we know it," the elder knight solemnly replied. Orimus unsheathed his sword and eyed the Dampire cautiously.

The mage held Xander in an embrace and focused on burning away the dark energy from his body. The Dampire squirmed in her arms, but she never let go. Selandra had a feeling that Xander knew what she was attempting to do. If he wanted to get away, the Dampire could easily break her hold.

"Let go," Xander painfully bit out. "I don't want to hurt you, Sel!"

"Help me then, damnit," the Peacekeeper sternly snapped. "Use your magic with me to flush the necromancer's dark taint from both of us."

Xander grunted in pain as his demonic side fought to take over. He could feel her magic warring with the darkness that seeped into his body. "What...do I...how do I...help?"

"Command any magic that isn't yours to flow out of your body. I have a stream of it flowing out of you, but it's not coming out fast enough. Put your intent in it. Make it leave and I'll help you build a shield that will keep it at bay."

"I should...leave…," Xander snarled, his voice etched with pain. "Don't want... to hurt... you, Sel..."

"Then do what I ask and I'll be safe. Do you trust me?"

The Dampire's eyes rapidly changed color as he bit out with a lot of effort, "Yes...Me?... Not sure..."

"Push it out. Let it flow through the channel I've made," Selandra ordered. Xander had sweat covering his visage, the effort not to succumb was becoming unbearable. He didn't want to allow it because the Dampire knew that he would kill the whole party, including his mage.

Xander focused the best that he could to push the dark energy from his body. It felt like it was trying to take over every cell, which his demonic side reveled in. Sweat beaded across his visage as Xander focused on pushing the dark energy out. Finally, it gave way and poured out of the Dampire like a swelling flooded river.

"Keep going," Selandra mentally encouraged him. *"Once it's fully out, I'll have a shielding in place that should keep it out of both of us."*

Xander grunted in acknowledgement. The more he watched it leave, Xander noticed that the dark energy kept finding its way back into him.

"Either put your shield up or be prepared for a long cycle of nonstop magic," Xander replied, the strain in his voice evident. *"I can't stop it. The hunger from my demonic side for this stuff is becoming unbearable!"*

The mage's eyes pulsated as she weaved her protective shielding around both of them. Selandra used the bond between them as a bridge to tether it in place. Both Garrett and Orimus shielded their eyes as the Peacekeeper's magic shined as bright as the sun for a few moments.

Xander's form sagged against Selandra as she finished the shield, his eyes were closed and his breathing was labored from exertion. She held him tightly as she whispered, "I got you, Xander. Rest now, you treacherous bastard."

Selandra glanced up at the two men and saw the assassin glaring with his sword in hand and the elder knight had a look of awe on his weathered face. He glanced over at Orimus and said, "I never thought I'd see the day. This mage truly has Xander under her control."

"I think that we should be going now that *that* unpleasantness is over," Selandra said as she urged her horse forward.

As she moved between them, Orimus callously spat, "Mere tricks to get us to lower our guard. I say we end the beast while he's out."

Selandra glared as her eyes glowed. "Try it, I dare you. Immolation will feel humane with what I plan on doing to you, assassin. Besides, what makes you think that he's out?"

"I told you that Orimus isn't that bright," Xander replied as he cast a side glance at the assassin with a smirk. "It's how he found himself in his current situation. Best keep your head down and your mouth shut, Orimus. I won't stop her because of your debt to me."

Chapter Sixteen

Several hours passed with little to no conversation. The little bit of light that snaked through the canopy dimmed as nightfall fast approached. The forest had an eerie silence, as if all the inhabitants were missing. Selandra wondered if they had moved on or were corrupted by the dark energy.

Despite the lack of life, the mage could feel eyes roaming over her. Selandra involuntarily shook, which caused Xander to closely eye her. He could hear her heart speeding up and so he asked, "What's got you on edge, Sel?"

"This place. Can't you hear it?"

"I hear nothing."

"Exactly," Selandra answered. "No birds chirping, no mating calls from insects. Nothing. And yet, we're being watched."

Garrett held up his hand as he brought his horse to a complete halt. He turned to the others as he pointed at his nose. "Does everyone smell that?"

A faint but pungent odor traveled in the light breeze. It consisted of sulphur, skunk, and rotten meat. When everyone nodded, the elder knight stated, "That is the unmistakable stench of the leapers. At least the wind is in our favor."

"Does it mean that we're nearing the mountains?" Orimus asked. His face scrunched in disgust from the pungent odor as he peered forward. "I don't see any signs of it."

"No," Garrett replied warily, "we are about an hour away from it. Leapers never come this far into the forest. They prefer the rocky terrain of the mountains to conceal themselves from unsuspecting travelers. This doesn't seem right to me. We shouldn't be smelling them."

"Xander," Selandra spoke as she looked around, "I know that you can see the best in the dark. Do you see them?"

"I'll need to get a better vantage point," Xander replied as he teleported away.

The Dampire appeared on a large branch high in the canopy. He surveyed the surrounding area and didn't see any signs of the leapers in the undergrowth, but their foul odor was thicker in the air. Xander looked around in the canopy and saw movement, though it was slight.

The creature was wrapped around the trunk of a birch tree, trying to mimic some of the massive thick vines that grew everywhere. It had pale green skin that was smooth and had a slight sheen. It had eight bulbous eyes similar to a spider on its elongated head and bony spikes protruding in different directions along the spine. Its mouth had teeth on the outside of its snout and jagged teeth poking out along the rest of the lips.

It had four muscular legs, the two front ones had a thick, two-foot-long bone spike protruding from the elbow joints and four lengthy claws at the end of each hand. The hind legs were stumpy, like a goat with no hooves, and had thicker claws that it used to dig into the side of the tree for support.

Xander looked at the rest of the trees and saw more of the same beasts stalking them. He was about to teleport when he heard movement coming from behind him, just above his head. Xander turned his head and was face to face with a leaper, its maw oozing with sickly yellow saliva. The leaper slashed at Xander's head, which he blocked with his arm. He countered it with a solid right hook to the creature's head, knocking it out of the tree.

"Eyes to the canopy!" Xander cried out as jumped off the branch, going after the leaper. "They're in the trees!"

Leapers cascaded down out of the canopy like a macabre hail storm of teeth and claws. Selandra barely had enough time to cast a protective shield as the nimble creatures rained down everywhere, but several managed to get inside with her.

The mage dismounted and unsheathed her sword, keeping a close eye on the predators. Selandra slashed in wide arches as the leapers flipped around, her sword barely making contact. Her horse cried out as it reared up on its hind legs, kicking wildly as one of the beasts harried it.

It shrieked as a couple of leapers landed on its back, impaling it with their vicious claws and cleaving chunks of flesh off. The mage couldn't bear seeing the horse suffering so she pulled out her staff and sent a blast of magic at it. The horse, along with the two leapers, burst into flames for a few seconds and then were reduced to a big pile of ash.

The mage was surrounded by three more leapers, each one snarling and snapping their maws. Selandra called out to the others, "Everyone, get in here. You'll be relatively safe in the shield!"

The mage wasn't sure if she could keep the leapers with her from disemboweling her or not, but she wasn't going to make it easy for them. She cast her spells at the creatures, but they seemed to anticipate and dodge her attacks. She felt confused, wondering why they weren't actually attacking her and then it dawned on the mage.

They're wearing me down to make for an easier kill.

Xander landed on top of one of the creatures. It snapped its maw at the Dampire, yet it couldn't bite him. The leaper got stuck in the ground on its back, its bony spikes were embedded in the thick roots from the tree. Xander pulled out his energy sword, the blade blazed brightly as he decapitated the beast.

Screaming caught the Dampire's attention as he saw Garrett's horse fall. The elder knight was pinned with one of his arms trapped under the weight of his dying horse as blood gushed from its throat. Garrett desperately tried to block the leaper's swipes as he cried out to the assassin, "Orimus! Help me, please!"

Orimus scoffed as he urged his steed forward, calling back, "Get yourself out of your own predicament, knight. I'm going to take the bounty with or without any of you!"

The Dampire glared at Orimus and his cowardice as he fled the fight. Xander felt conflicted whether to assist the elder knight or join Selandra in her fight. He sent a blast of energy from his weapon at the leapers, but it was too late. One of the leapers managed to pin his arm while a second one viciously bit down on Garrett's face, taking most of it off.

The blast killed the unsuspecting predators so Xander teleported himself in the protective shielding, next to Selandra. He could see fatigue on her face from all the magical exertion so he said, "Shield yourself and allow me to deal with these pests."

"I can take care-"

"Just do as I ask, Sel," Xander growled as he walked towards the leapers. "Garrett is dead and Orimus has fled. I'm not going to lose you too."

The mage nodded irritability as she pulled her shielding in closer to her body. She sat down on the ground to rest and conserve her energy but kept her weapons at the ready, in case Xander got in trouble.

The Dampire had his weapon in hand and a malicious grin on his visage. "Come on, then. Let's see what you got."

The leapers circled Xander, lunging and leaping. The Dampire teleported himself next to the closest creature and slashed off its legs. The leaper let out a high pitch screech as it rolled around on the ground. Xander glared at the other two leapers, challenging them to attack as he tossed the wounded leaper at them.

"You beasties care to do the dance of death?" Xander mocked. The leapers roared as they jumped at him, their deadly claws coming down at him like a mass of blades. The Dampire twirled around, slashing and stabbing any creature that got within striking distance. Selandra watched on and wondered if this is how he fought during the war. His movements were fluid and he swayed like he was dancing to music that only he could hear.

It was beautiful and bloody, just like the Dampire. She now understood why he didn't want her in this fight. Xander's eyes were focused and it seemed like he was in a meditative state, seeing every movement of the leapers before it happened. Xander surprised the Peacekeeper with a quick blast to her left. Selandra saw the body of a leaper split in two near her shielding. Xander kept on going, completely unfazed by the assaults happening all around him.

More of the agile creatures encroached on Xander, but each one met the same fate. By the time the attack was done, nothing but gore and body parts were strewn everywhere. Xander, much to the mage's surprise, was relatively clean. He extinguished the energy blade and sheathed the hilt as he walked over to the fallen knight. Xander kneeled down and placed his hands on his body and teleported away with him.

Selandra dropped her shielding and stood up. She walked over to the dead horse and retrieved a water gourd. The mage took several gulps of water as Xander reappeared. He walked over and asked, "Are you well, Sel?"

"Just a little fatigued." She looked around and felt deflated. "Looks like we're on foot from here on out."

"Nonsense," the Dampire replied as he took the mage by her hand. "Orimus isn't that far from here. I can tell because I've tasted his blood."

"Exactly how many people have you fed on? Why did you take Garrett's dead body away?" Selandra probed.

Xander coldly retorted, "Too many to count. He deserves a proper burial. A promise made; a promise kept. He's where he needs to be, though Garrett should be alive, no thanks to Orimus. I plan on having a little chat with that spineless git. That said, let's pay the bastard a visit."

As Selandra nodded and firmly gripped his hand, Xander teleported them away.

Chapter Seventeen

"Huh," Xander flatly stated, feeling confused. "The prick should be here, but I don't see him."

"It's okay Xander," Selandra replied with a smirk. "Nobody's perfect. Maybe you're picking up on something else?"

"His blood called me to this area for a reason," the Dampire stated as he looked around. A rustling in the underbrush to their right caused them both to unsheathe their weapons. Stomping on the ground nearby, along with the neighing, let them know that it was a horse. Selandra peered through the weeds and saw that it was the same one that the assassin fled away on.

The mage approached the steed with her hands out. The horse reared up on its hind legs, appearing distressed and terrified. Selandra kept her distance with her eyes locked on the horse's bulbous black eyes.

"Shhhh," the Peacekeeper calmly spoke, trying to placate the beast as she pulled out an apple. "It's okay. You're safe. I'm here now."

She extended her arm out, offering the apple as a way to get the horse to trust her. The horse settled down with all of its hooves on the ground. Its ears twitched several times as it approached the mage. Selandra wondered if the leapers had caught up with Orimus and killed him, which didn't seem right.

Why kill the rider and leave the horse alive?

The horse timidly sniffed at the apple before snatching it from Selandra's hand. As it crunched on the fruit, the Peacekeeper reached up and stroked its head and long neck, murmuring softly. She channeled a bit of calming magic with each caress of her hand, slowly relaxing the horse. It nuzzled its head against the mage, snorting.

"Nicely done, Sel," Xander said as he stood next to her. "At least we won't be on foot now."

"This doesn't make sense. This is Orimus's horse, but he isn't here. Did you discover anything about this area?"

"I did, but first," he motioned to the horse, "let's mount up and I'll show you what I found."

She glanced at the Dampire as she grasped the reign. The mage grabbed the saddle horn and hoisted herself up on the horse's back. She adjusted herself as Xander appeared in front of her. He nestled his tiny form against her warm body and pointed. "Head back to the trail. There's much to see."

Selandra urged the steed forward. It seemed reluctant at first, but it moved in the direction cautiously. On the trail, Xander motioned to the ground. "I found a pool of blood that belongs to Orimus. Best I can tell is that he was knocked from his horse by something. Probably cracked his pathetic skull on that rock down there. That's why I was led to this area. The fool hurt himself."

"If that's the case, then where is he?" Selandra asked as she looked around.

"That's just it, he isn't here. I found remains of the leapers that hunted him, but not Orimus."

"So, he was knocked off his horse and he managed to slay the beasts? Did he wander off after his fight?" the mage spoke aloud as the dead creatures came into view. Something didn't feel right. The wounds inflicted on the leapers ran deep, like a large cleaver was used to kill them.

"He didn't kill these predators," Xander chimed in. He teleported down to the ground and pointed at one of the dead carcasses. "Orimus is armed but not with the weapon that did this. A cleaver axe downed these beasts. Be a dear and illuminate the area for me."

"Why? You can see just fine in the darkness."

Xander nodded. "This is true, but the light isn't for me. I'm going to show you what I see. But there's a chance that something might catch your pristine eyesight."

Selandra nodded as she pulled out her staff. The crystal tip glowed as a small orb of light floated effortlessly in the air, illuminating a radius of twenty feet. The Dampire roamed around, paying meticulous attention to the ground. "There's fresh tracks all over the place. Leapers, his horse, but none belonging to Orimus."

The mage pointed down at a patch of loose earth. "Are those divots fresh tracks?"

Xander leaned down to examine the spot. "Yes. These are the cloven hoof prints of the goatmen. I surmise that the buffoon rode his steed through here and got ambushed by them. He fell off his horse and then the goatmen slaughtered the pursuing leapers."

"Which way did they go and why did they take Orimus?" Selandra asked as Xander reappeared in front of her. The Dampire pointed towards a narrow game trail. "Their tracks veer off the path. I suggest that we leave him to his fate and press on."

"That's cold, Xander," the mage admonished as she steered the horse down the game trail, "even for you. I know that you don't like the man but we need to at least try to rescue him."

"He deserves a fate worse than death. He abandoned Garrett and left him to die. Imagine if he didn't come along. It might have been you under the horse."

Selandra kept quiet as she silently extinguished her light. The game trail was both winding and well-worn on a steep incline, which made their trek go slower as darkness encased the forest. The Dampire remained alert, watching their surroundings for any kind of threats. The smell of decay permeated the stagnant air. Xander wondered if they were getting closer to a nest of leapers.

Selandra slowed the horse to a complete halt and whispered, "Do you see anything?"

"No, but I do hear muttering chatter coming from the top of the ridge. I imagine that we're about to meet the goatmen."

The mage nodded. "Have you had many encounters with them before?"

"I have. Best keep your wits about you. They may attempt to take you away for breeding purposes. I'll do my best to prevent it from happening."

"What a lovely thought," Selandra flatly stated.

"I have a plan for it, so I need you to play along. Since I'm part demon, they shouldn't be too territorial...much," the Dampire replied as he looked up at the ridgeline. Several goatmen were peering down in their direction. "We've been spotted. I guess that it's high time we introduce ourselves to this clan."

Selandra could barely see them, but could hear them talking with excitement as they alerted the others. She encouraged their steed to move once more. The horse fearfully whinnied as a small group of goatmen marched down towards them. Xander looked up at the mage and said, "Wait here. Give me a few minutes to sort this out."

He teleported away before Selandra could respond. She watched as he startled the goatmen by appearing about five feet in front of them. Oddly enough, the creatures didn't attack the Dampire. Selandra strained to hear what they were saying. Xander motioned to the Peacekeeper, but kept on speaking to the group. The goatmen nodded in unison as Xander reappeared on the horse.

"They're going to escort us into their den to meet their queen," Xander said.

As she got their steed moving again, Selandra asked, "What did you say to them?"

"I told them to keep their little *kids* in their proverbial pants when around you."

"And they agreed to this?" Selandra asked.

"Not at first, but when I told them my name, they wised up quickly. And it's why we're going to see this queen of theirs."

"You don't sound sure."

The Dampire stroked his chin as they approached the group. "Goatmen don't have any form of monarchy system that I know of, so call me curious. I say this because there's no goat females. Hence, the reason for snatching women for breeding."

The mage tugged her hood up to hide her disgust. "That's barbaric."

The group of goatmen surrounded them and marched in tandem as Xander replied, "This is true, Sel, but it's their way of life. They view you as nothing more than livestock. Something to breed and bear their offspring. Trust me when I say, it's not a pleasant experience. It's deplorable, but it's the only method they know to perpetuate their species."

"So, what happens to the women? Do they get to leave eventually?"

"Some escape, but it's rare. They get tied down and get bred repeatedly by each clan member. Some get the distinction of being caretakers for the little ones for being barren, but it doesn't stop the breeding. It just becomes less frequent. Most of the women end up dying, either from too much breeding or suicide."

Selandra glanced over at their escorts. The goatmen were about seven feet tall, including their long, jagged black horns. They had the visage of a deformed goat with black eyes with red slits. Each one had well defined muscles on both their broad chests and arms that resembled a human. They wore no clothing of any kind. Their thick legs had coarse, matted black hair that covered their hips and massive hooves much thicker than a normal goat. Some carried crudely crafted bows and arrows, while others had massive cleaver axes in their hands caked in dry blood.

As they reached the top of the ridgeline, a small hamlet appeared about a hundred yards away. Huts and other structures around the small settlement seemed old and man-made, which meant that it was abandoned and forgotten long ago. The goatmen claimed it as their own, many were keeping a watchful eye on the newcomers.

Muffled screaming and wailing of women filled the air, causing the mage to shutter. She felt a small hand touching her thigh as Xander said, "I won't let that be your fate. You're mine to play with and I don't share."

Selandra nodded slowly but everything about this place unnerved her. She caught a glimpse in one of the old stables and gasped when she saw what the Dampire meant by breeding. Women were held down in place by ropes or in crudely crafted stocks, either on their backs or bellies, while other women were shackled to the walls. The goatmen didn't discriminate on age, it seemed to the mage. Some were about her age while others looked to be barely in their teens.

One of the captive women locked her hooded eyes on Selandra and mouthed out as a goatman was roughly rutting her, "Kill me..."

"Now is not the time for thrilling heroics, Sel. Though I must admit, this place is peculiar," Xander said, sensing the Peacekeeper's anger.

"This whole place is peculiar and wrong and you know it," the mage hissed quietly, unsure if the creatures escorting them could understand her.

"This is true but as I said before, this is their way of life, but it's different from what I've seen before."

"How so?"

"They seem more organized and orderly. A normal encampment wouldn't utilize the structures for breeding. They would simply take you wherever they want," the Dampire replied as he contemplated while stroking his chin. "I wonder if it has anything to do with their so-called *queen*. Goatmen aren't *this* discreet."

The mage could feel the lustful gazes of the other goatmen around the village eyeing her like she was going to be the next breed. Their path led to a small cavernous opening in the side of the mountain. The entrance to the cave was heavily guarded by goatmen and had several leapers chained nearby.

Xander was impressed. All the guards had to do was unleash their pet leapers and the threat would easily be neutralized. The lead goatman held up his hand, halting everyone in place. The creature approached the guards by himself, leaving the Dampire and the mage with the group. The creatures spoke in what Selandra could tell was a variation of a demonic dialect, occasionally their vocalizations sounded hoarse, like what a regular goat would make.

One of the goatmen came over and took the reins from Selandra and spoke in broken English as it pointed. "Off. Beast here. Walk queen."

"This is our stop, Sel. We walk from here," Xander stated as he slipped off the horse. He reached up and assisted the Peacekeeper down. The goatman grunted as he led their steed over to a nearby spring that trickled down from the mountain. The remaining goatmen surrounded them and escorted them into the cave.

Chapter Eighteen

The cavern layout was meticulously carved out and expansive, the telltale signs of dwarven craftsmanship at some point in time. The torch sconces on the wall were nothing more than long bones with broken skulls affixed on top for the fire to be cradled in and encased by rib cages. It gave an eerie atmosphere as the light danced around, casting many shadows.

The tunnel had a few meek and broken women tending to whatever task they had, none had any clothes on and were adorned with many scars and bruises. The rock walls were damp and glistened as tiny trickles of water seeped in.

"Stay close to me, Sel," Xander mentally warned. *"I'm not sure what to expect, but if things get out of hand, I'll get us both to safety."*

They turned to walk up a staircase that had been carved out by hand. The sound of hooves clacking on the stone echoed in the small tunnel. Xander was feeling bored as the stone stairs descended down and called out,

"Are we there yet or does your queen reside in the depths of the mountain?"

Selandra heard one of the goatmen chattering to the Dampire, but then she felt a callous hand touching her back, trailing down slowly before roughly grabbing her ass.

The mage twirled around and quickly admonished the creature. "Hands off, beast! I'm not here for your pleasure!"

The goatman either didn't understand her or simply ignored her as it shoved Selandra against the cold stone wall. It snatched her by the wrists to prevent the mage from grabbing her weapons. The goatman grunted as it pressed its body against hers, the smell of sulphur and rot wafted from its breath as it snaked its black tongue out to lick her face.

The Peacekeeper cried out, "Stop it!"

A sickening crack reverberated in the stairwell as Xander stood on the goatman's back, breaking its neck easily. As the creature fell limply on the stairs, the Dampire eyed the other goatmen with his energy blade ignited as he stood on the body. "The next one that so much as glances at Selandra, I'll send you to meet your friend here. Now tell me the truth, do you cretins actually have a queen or not?"

The goatman stared at Xander, chattering in their demonic dialect. One stepped forward and kneeled down before him. To Selandra, she could almost hear it pleading with the Dampire in its tone. Xander nodded but his anger didn't ebb as he barked, "None shall follow behind us. I want all of you where I can see you or I *will* show you *my* demonic lust for blood."

The goatman grunted as they moved to the front to lead the way. Xander walked next to the mage and asked, "You okay, Sel?"

"I'm fine," she replied curtly as she marched in tandem with the Dampire. "Let's meet this queen and move on to the necromancer."

Xander glanced up at her, noting that her bottom lip was quivering. He could tell that Selandra was upset and with good reason, but he let her be. The stairwell opened up to a larger chamber room with several tunnels on both sides and straight ahead was a heavy oak door. The door was protected by more goatmen sentries that snapped to attention as they saw who their brethren had with them. Chattering ensued between the creatures while Xander listened intently.

"Interesting," he said as a sly grin crossed his visage.

"What's happening?"

"If I heard them correctly, I think that I know who their queen is but I won't be sure until we gain entrance to her chamber."

"Another *friend* I should worry about?" Selandra asked as one of the sentries reached over and pulled the heavy oak door open.

"Possibly. It will depend on her mood and whether she'll like seeing me once again."

As the goatmen motioned for them to enter, the Peacekeeper sarcastically muttered, "Oh, that's comforting to know."

They walked into the queen's chamber as a goatman ran ahead. The creature went into an antechamber as the heavy oak door was closed behind them. Moments later, the goatman and a young-looking woman stepped into the chamber. The queen had a full, curvy figure and her skin was pale and showed no signs of blemishes. Her hair was a deep crimson and was thick and curly. She wore thick brown leggings along with ankle high black boots and a navy-blue blouse that had a hole strategically placed to accentuate her ample breasts.

The female had slanted crimson eyes that bore into the Peacekeeper as she examined her like a predator would its next meal. The queen's gaze left Selandra and fell on Xander, which caused the corners of her lips to curl up. "Xander Bane. I never thought I'd see you again. Tell me, how's your father doing these days?"

"Vivian," the Dampire nodded slightly, "You of all people should know how that loving relationship is. I paid him a visit recently."

Vivian chuckled. "And how did it turn out? Is he no more?"

"No, he still lives for now but he's wounded for trying to kill Selandra here." He motioned to the mage.

"Vivian." The mage nodded as Xander did.

"Hmm," the queen spoke as she circled around the Peacekeeper, slowly assessing her, "it's not like you to be so protective over living flesh. What are you doing with this Peacekeeper? Is she your personal blood slave?"

Selandra could sense that the queen was a vampire, the smell of decay permeated the air around her as the queen moved. The mage felt uncomfortable under her crimson stare, wondering if she would try and bite her.

"I'm an indentured servant of the Peacekeepers of Le'orn for breaking the Vampire Pact. Selandra here is my handler because you know how trustworthy I can be."

Vivian smirked. "Handler, you say? I could kill her for you and free you from their hold over you."

"You can try," Selandra retorted, her hand touching the hilt of her sword, "but Xander won't allow it. I may be his handler, but I'm also his partner."

"What she says is the truth," the Dampire replied as he stepped in front of the vampire with his arms across his chest. "My father tried to kill her and lost an arm for his assault. I won't allow her to be slain by the queen of a bunch of goatmen. Is that how you came to rule over the goatmen, I wonder? Spreading those legs like butter when they come a knocking?"

"You know I'm not *that* easy," Vivian replied with a huff of indignation. "I'm not so easily swayed by beautiful words. Many have tried and ended up impaled on my fangs."

"This is true, you've been around for what, twelve centuries? I'm sure not many have had the chance to bed you. That might explain why you're such a grumpy old bat!"

The queen crossed her arms across her chest. "Charming as ever, I see. Now tell me what is the reason for this intrusion?"

"We're here to collect on a bounty, but I'm sure you figured that out," Xander replied as he walked over and looked up at the vampire.

Vivian hissed as she slipped into a fighting stance, her razor-sharp fingernails extended by three inches. "I see. I suppose that it was only a matter of time before the vampire council sent you to fetch my head!"

"The only heads I'd take would be those on the vampire council," Selandra retorted as she stepped up beside the Dampire confidently and unconsciously placed a hand on top of Xander's head. "Like he said, they tried to kill us because of their arrangement with the necromancer. All we want from you is information about her, nothing more, Vivian."

The queen glared intently at the mage, trying to gauge if this was the truth. She glanced at the Dampire when he added, "Do you really believe that those buffoons would send *me* after you? We're here for her, not a rogue vampire."

"A rogue?" Selandra uttered, feeling confused. "What does that mean, Xander?"

"It means," Vivian replied as she sauntered over to a comfortable plush chair, "I'm a wanted criminal for refusing the mandate to fight during the Fae war. Much like sweet little Xander, I'm an outcast amongst the vampire community. Tell me, are you the only ones hunting for her?"

"First things first, Vivian," Xander asked. "How did you become the queen to these goatmen?"

"It wasn't something that I sought out," Vivian said as she thrummed her fingers on her chair. "I was on the run both during and after the war. Being shunned isn't a pleasant lifestyle. I had to feed on anything that I came across. You name it, I fed on it. Once I heard about the Vampire Pact, all I wanted to do was walk in the sunlight and be done with myself. As fate intervened, I stumbled upon this little hole. Can you imagine being a lone female in a den of a bunch of horny goatmen?"

"I have a vivid image of what you mean," the mage replied with a shudder.

"I decided to go out fighting. At least if they wanted me, these beasts needed to earn it. I must've slaughtered several dozen of them before they backed down. In a mass unity, all the goatmen dropped their weapons and bowed down to me. I wasn't sure what to make of this, but one of them stepped towards me and pointed at me and uttered, 'Queen. Ours.' in that rudimentary way it spoke. They brought me food and different drinks as an offering, but as you know, I can't stomach either. It was amusing seeing those goatman working so hard to please me. I saw that they had women here for their own needs so I struck a bargain with them on the perfect offering. I feed on all their captive women they catch, which makes them easier for breeding."

"You're quite plump and well fed," Xander stated as he sniffed the air. "Tell me, have you fed in the last hour or so?"

"I have." Vivian smirked as she licked her fangs. "He was the first man I've had in a long while. A friend of yours, I take it?"

"No, but Orimus was a part of our party," Selandra answered.

"If you killed him," the Dampire grinned as he sarcastically added, "then I would suffer a terrible wound that, dare I say, will never heal. I wouldn't have the heart to avenge him."

The mage rolled her eyes as the queen let out a belly laugh that echoed throughout the chamber. Vivian, still laughing as she wiped crimson tears away, said, "Damn, I've missed you and your brutal honesty, Xander Bane. I've not had a good laugh in ages. Believe it or not, you were the one who caused it too. But to answer your query, no, I didn't kill this Orimus, but I did put him on that path."

"What do you mean by that?" Selandra asked, but had her own suspicions as to where the assassin was going.

"Does it truly matter? I can tell that neither of you have any love or loyalty to the man, unlike you two have for each other," Vivian answered as her glazed darted between Xander and the Peacekeeper. A genuine smile broke over her soft, flawless visage. "Did your father not realize what you two have? The bond that you share? It's beautiful to see it, but even more so that you have it, Xander. A magnificent 'fuck you!' to Vestal."

"You can see it?" Selandra blurted out. A wave of shock cascaded over her face.

"Vampires can't *see* things like that. How is this possible?" Xander asked and then added, "And answer her previous question? Where is the prick?"

"The necromancer. All roads lead back to her. I drained him and had him taken to Morana so she can do whatever she wants with him. Part of another arrangement like I have here."

Chapter Nineteen

"What arrangement might that be," Xander asked as he narrowed his tear shaped eyes. The queen stood up and sauntered over to a large table. Vivian picked up a piece of parchment and handed it to Xander. He examined the document for a few minutes before handing it over to Selandra.

The mage was astonished with each passage that she read. She looked up at the vampire and said, "Seriously? She can do this?"

"Indeed, my dear," Vivian replied as she took the parchment back and tossed it back on the table. "She wanted me to join her in her little war by offering me her blood slaves as payment, but I refused. You must understand that I don't care much for war and all the drama that comes with it so she made a different deal with me. I supply her with able bodies, either dead or on the brink of death and she would grant me magical abilities that no other vampire possesses, with the exception of Xander here. Essentially, Morana transformed me into the first vampire mage."

"Why would she do that?" Selandra blurted out. "What does Morana have to gain from this?"

Vivian walked over and got behind Selandra. The mage stiffened as the queen wrapped her arms around her like a lover's embrace. "Morana does whatever she wants because she can. This is her way of paying for my services. She gains an unstoppable army and I get to *see* my prey using her magic. We're linked to each other, which means that what I see and hear, so does she. Do you know how valuable that kind knowledge can be when preparing for a grand scale war? Morana isn't some two-bit mage. She's far older and wiser than anyone on this planet, with the exception of her brothers of course."

"Aren't you betraying her by saying all of this?" Selandra asked as she pushed away from the vampire. The mage noticed that Vivian's eyes went from crimson red to black. Her facial features distorted slightly, morphing as though someone else had taken over the vampire's body.

"Vivian can say whatever she wants here because I know what lies in her mind. No secrets can be kept from me once our deal was struck." The voice of the vampire changed, sounding both hoarse and sultry at the same time.

"Morana, I presume," Xander said as he boldly stepped in front of Selandra. "I guess if what you say is true, then you know why we're searching for you?"

The possessed vampire chuckled. *"I do, but I don't fear either of you. Not like the others do. I'm expecting you both to come before me. I have no quarrel with either of you, but if you want to fight, so be it. I'd rather have you two as my allies, given the influence that my brother has over both of you."*

"Who is your brother?" the Dampire inquired.

"Come to my domain and I shall reveal all. This form of communication is taxing on a mortal body, but even more so on my undead child here. I make an oath not to harm either of you in exchange for information. Information about the one that

placed those painful wardings on you, Xander, and the bond you two share. Do you accept this parley?"

At once, Vivian dropped hard to her knees, clutching her stomach. Breathing heavily but not looking up, she asked, "Do you agree to her terms?"

"Can we discuss-"

Vivian cut off the mage as she jerked her head up. Her eyes showed both pain and the unmistakable signs of hunger as bloody tears trickled down her cheeks. "Yes or no!"

"Yes," Xander replied as he got mere inches from her face and caressed the queen's cheek. "If you promise not to feed on *my* mage, I'll fetch a meal for you."

"I can't guarantee her safety and you know this," Vivian vehemently hissed, her eyes pleading with the Dampire. "I don't want to kill your lover. You deserve a happy, peaceful life. I don't want to add to your hardship. I have blood coming to me as we speak. I need you to remain where you are, Xander."

The Dampire cupped his hands on the vampire queen's face, his eyes locked with hers. "Just focus on me, Vivian. No sudden movements, Sel."

"What's happening with her?"

"It appears that the necromancer wasn't lying about her communication being taxing on the body. Vivian is feeling the need to feed, but more like a feral vampire. It used to be rare to see, but it's a byproduct of what the Vampire Pact put most vampires through. A hunger so strong that if the vampire doesn't feed, it will consume its own body. If she sees you, you'll be dead in less than a minute."

The door to the chamber was forcefully opened as several goatmen barged in. Each one was carrying a woman in their arms, wailing loudly as they kicked and hit their captors futilely. Xander teleported next to Selandra, quickly turning her away as the queen of the goatmen tore into each woman viscously.

"Don't look, Sel. It's not a pretty sight," the Dampire said as he held her hand. The mage squeezed her eyes shut, trying to shut out the screaming and whimpers coming from Vivian's victims.

Soon the chamber grew quiet. The female vampire walked past Selandra and the Dampire and sat down on her chair. She licked the remnants of blood off of her lips and said, "My apologies for my feeding. It couldn't be helped." She glanced at the goatmen and ordered, "Take those bodies to Morana."

The goatman uttered unintelligibly as they scooped up the women and hastily retreated from the chamber. Xander eyed the queen for a moment and then proclaimed, "The necromancer gave you a psychic connection with these beasts."

"An added bonus from her dark gifts for me. Loyalty is rewarded well by her. Something that is non-existent within the vampire council," Vivian replied as she stood up and crossed the distance between her and the mage. "She is as cunning as she is ancient. Morana has many secrets that she will reveal to you and then, you'll have to make a decision."

"Let me guess," Selandra responded, her hand inching towards the hilt of her sword, "join her or die. Is that it?"

"That would be telling," Vivian cooed as she brushed her hand along the Peacekeeper's cheek slowly. "Just know that there's more going on than either of you can comprehend. Like a chess board with hidden pieces and we're the pawns."

"That much is evident," the Dampire replied as he squeezed Selandra's hand.

Vivian smiled down at him and said, "If this one breaks your heart, you know where you can find me, Xander."

Selandra fumed, but then she heard Xander in her mind. *I'll explain later, Sel.*

"There's no physical way to get to Morana. You'll have to portal your way to her."

"I'll need her magical signature to do that," Selandra said and then realized something. "Exactly how are your goatmen getting the bodies to her? They don't create portals, do they?"

"I see why you fancy this one. A clever one, she is," Vivian stated as she walked over to the wall, beckoning them to follow. She pulled out a small dagger and held it out by the blade. Selandra took it as the queen explained, "Do you see this symbol on the wall? These are her blood portals. Just trace your blood in the symbol, say her name three times, and a gateway will form. The goatman have a difficult time saying her name so they have special ones that only they can access."

"Will you be coming along?" The mage asked.

"I'm not allowed to at this time. Morana is waiting for you. Don't be a fool and deny her, Xander. She has much to offer."

"More like control over us too, I imagine," Xander replied, rolling his eyes.

"If we do this," the Peacekeeper suspiciously pointed out, "Morana will have control over us whether we like it or not."

The Dampire looked up at the mage as Vivian chuckled. "She knows her magic. What a powerful pair you two make. Selandra is correct. It's a safety precaution, in case someone breaches her domain. Despite having the blood of the assassin in you, Xander, you would be repelled from entering. This is the only way that she's told me of. I'm sure there's other ways."

"Like Merrick had over you earlier. I hope that she has an explanation for her mage's actions," Xander stated, knowing that the necromancer was listening. He snatched the dagger from Selandra's hand and sliced his finger. He traced his bleeding finger through the sigil and muttered the necromancer's name three times. The sigil glowed bright for a moment and then it absorbed the Dampire's blood. A black portal hazily materialized on the wall to the left of the sigil.

Vivian ordered, "Now your turn, mage. It won't let you through unless payment is given."

Selandra took the dagger from Xander and cut her finger and repeated the same blood magic. She wasn't fond of letting others have control over her magically, especially after what Merrick did to her. Once she finished, the sigil flared up and accepted her blood. The black portal fully coalesced and the Dampire grinned as he walked through. "See you on the other side, Sel."

Before Selandra could follow, the queen grabbed her and held her tightly. She leaned in and whispered, "Xander Bane is *mine*. If you do hurt him," the vampire stuck the mage's bloody finger in her mouth, "I'll hunt you down and let my army breed you day and night until you're on the brink of death. Then I'll turn you so you can endure more breeding for the rest of your miserable life. Got it, mage?"

"Let me go or he will get suspicious," Selandra calmly replied. "You have what you want, now let me join him or he will end you."

"I should end you for that comment," Vivian hissed, her fangs mere inches from the Peacekeeper's neck, "but Morana says to leave you be, for now."

The vampire released Selandra from her death grip and backed away. Selandra glanced over her shoulder at her before stepping through the portal. Vivian sneered at her, like she was disgusted by the mage. "Go. Be with him, but remember what I said."

Selandra felt an overwhelming sense of vertigo as she passed through the portal and then she found herself on the ground, writhing in pain. She looked over and saw Xander on the ground, his demonic side showing as he felt the pain.

"What the fuck is wrong with the portal," the Dampire snarled, pounding the ground with his fist.

"Blood payment," Selandra cried out. "It will pass. I hope..."

Xander struggled to his feet and stood up, despite the pain. He shuffled over and looked down at his mage. Tears streamed down her cheeks; her jaw was clenched tightly as she groaned. The Dampire breathed heavily, his anger seething as he watched on helplessly.

"Damn conjurers," was all that Xander could say. Selandra's body finally stilled, her painful moans turned into a whimper. The Dampire sat down next to her as she rolled over and wrapped her arms around his waist.

"What is it with you conjurers and painful wardings?" Xander spoke as he rubbed the mage's back.

"Protection," Selandra muttered with her eyes closed. "Though I will say that was the most extreme type that I've ever endured. If we weren't welcome here, it would have killed us."

"Vivian is right. There's more going on than meets the eye. Just rest, Sel. I'll keep watch over you."

The mage bitterly asked, "Speaking of that leech, what's the story between you two? Are you two old lovers?"

Xander snorted, causing the mage to open her eyes and look at him. He appeared to be reverting back to his normal self with a look of irritation on his regal visage. "We were promised to each other long ago. My father and Vivian had bartered a deal to secure more territory to hunt on if he would grant her his next sired vampire. When I was born, my father was furious and wanted to destroy me but both my mother and Vivian intervened. Vestal stated that I was an abomination and should be destroyed. Vivian argued that I was the payment that they had agreed to in their bargain. He wasn't having it, stating that he meant he would sire a human for her. Sire also included bearing a child, something that he didn't consider possible since he's an ancient vampire."

"Are you saying that vampires can't have children?" Selandra asked. She glanced down at her own belly with sadness at the thought of never having the Dampire's child.

"You would be correct," Xander replied with a laugh. "Now imagine my father's reaction. He was shocked and livid, from what I heard. I shouldn't be here and yet, I am. Apparently, having sex with a succubus changes the equation for vampires. Somehow, my mother managed to take his dead sperm and create life with it with her sex magic. At least, that's the working theory in the vampire community."

"Would you want to?" The mage gulped hard. "Have you ever thought about having a child of your own?"

"I've no clue if it's possible. If that's what you're brooding over at the moment, I can't say for sure. I'll not give you false hope in this matter. You should be with someone that can give you this. As I said before, I'll only bring you pain and suffering, Sel."

"I don't care. You may keep trying to push me away, but I refuse to give up on you, or us for that matter, Xander. Vivian threatened to torture me if I ever broke your heart."

"For some reason, she's stuck on the notion that I'm her intended after all these centuries," Xander replied. "She's threatened many people, including my father. I wouldn't worry about her. With the bounty on her head, Vivian is forced to stay put."

"She-she tasted my blood. Before I stepped through the portal. With her new magical abilities, she might be able to find me with little effort."

Xander growled, "She bit you? I guarantee that when we've finished our business here with this Morana, I'll bring you Vivian and I'll help you personally watch her burn in the sunlight."

"She suckled the blood from my finger." Selandra shrugged. "I think she's jealous of the bond that we share. I believe that she would've gladly snapped my neck if she could've gotten away with it. Guess I should add her and the goatmen to the ever-growing list of people who want me dead."

"If the portal was still active, I would go back through and slaughter them all without hesitation, Sel. But since it's gone," the Dampire said as he stood up with his hands out to help Selandra up, "let's go pay a visit to the necromancer."

Selandra stood up and winced from the residual pain. She looked down at Xander and asked, "Am I worth the trouble? At least Vivian could spend an eternity with you. Maybe she's right. I'll just break your heart because I'm not an immortal like you."

Xander teleported himself onto the mage's back and whispered, "I'll take my chances with you, Sel. I don't know if it's the bond or not, but know that I'd gladly raze this world just to keep you safe from harm. If that doesn't scare you off, then you're a fool, Mage."

"If these events keep unfolding," Selandra replied between kisses, "you might end up doing just that, if war breaks out once again."

"Be prepared for it, Sel," the Dampire replied coldly. "Because you'll see a side of me that you never knew possible."

"And what side is that?"

Xander looked her in the eyes and flatly stated, "Death incarnate."

Chapter Twenty

Xander looked around at their surroundings and noticed two things: one was that the necromancer wasn't in the Capricorn Range at all. Her dwelling was somewhere deep underground, or so it seemed. The ground was mostly rock and any soil gave off a putrid aroma. Two, the air was stagnant and poor quality, the scent of death and decay permeated it like a foul perfume.

Shuffling footsteps caught their attention as a small cluster of reanimated corpses ambled towards them. Some had various stages of decomposition, from rotting flesh and exposed bones and muscles while others looked so unblemished that you couldn't tell if they were dead or alive. The group consisted of humans, fae, elves, and several trolls.

Selandra gasped when she saw a few mages in the group, knowing full well that they died long ago, their Peacekeeper uniforms were tattered and torn, but still recognizable. A female mage in a dirty hunter green cloak that had been slashed up by a sword stepped up to Selandra and put her hand on her shoulder, causing her to flinch. "Selandra, why do you recoil from me? Is that truly you? I thought I'd never see you again."

The woman's voice seemed hollow, but the mage recognized her right away, despite the decay. "Tessa?"

The undead mage beamed a radiant smile. "Yes, dear. Have you been keeping up with your lessons?"

Selandra motioned to the Dampire as she replied, "Lately, no. This one has been pushing me more than any of my teachers ever could."

Tessa cocked an eyebrow as smirked. "Including me?"

"Selandra is skilled and beyond the inadequate teachings of the spire," Xander stated, causing the mage to blush. "If you were once her teacher, then I'd say that you taught her well."

"Is that a fact, Xander?" Tessa countered, studying the Dampire.

"If I were to go to war again," Xander looked the undead mage in her cloudy eyes, "there's no other mage that I'd want by my side. How do you know my name?"

Tessa chuckled as she stepped away from Selandra. "It's undeniable to not recognize the one known as the Abominable Butcher. I recall our encounter during the war. Obviously, it didn't end well for me."

Selandra blurted, "You killed Tessa?"

Xander shrugged his little shoulders. "We danced and she didn't survive. It happens in war. I honestly don't recall fighting her."

"You killed all of us on that day," a male mage spoke up. Selandra was surprised that none of her former Peacekeeper colleagues held a grudge or animosity towards the Dampire. The mage sounded calm, his voice flat and devoid of emotion. "Like you said, it was a time of war. Not all survive, but we do remember that day well."

Tessa cocked her head to the side and asked, "Tell me why you reacted to my touch?

It's not like you to do that when I was with you years ago."

"I'm sorry, master," Selandra replied, feeling uncomfortable, "It's not you. We-we came across Merrick not that long ago."

"I see," Tessa said flatly as she turned on heels. She motioned for them to follow her. "Here's the main drawback of our existence. We have an obsession that we must have something that we loved when we were alive. Myself, it's daisies as you can see." She removed her hood, showing her stringy hair covered in the little flowers. Selandra warmly smiled as many memories flooded her mind.

"Merrick, unfortunately, is drawn to you. You're his main obsession. He should be at Crimson Pass, not out tracking you down. I do apologize for it. I can see that he's affected you greatly. I promise to punish him when he returns."

"That may take a while," Xander replied as they walked down a well-worn road, many of the reanimated corpses stood in total silence. The number of undead looked massive and awaiting instructions as they stood in mute silence. "Merrick is in a dungeon back in Le'orn. He tried to kill her when he couldn't convert her to your cause."

"I was afraid of that." Tessa sighed as she looked over at the mage. "At least he's where he should be."

Selandra nodded but kept quiet as they marched down the path. Xander couldn't help observing just how massive the necromancer's army was. The number of different races that were mixed together bespoke of how formidable it would be if she unleashed them all. Using the mages, and possibly other magical creatures, meant that Morana could manage her war from the safety of this place.

"Where exactly are we, Tessa? This place feels off for some reason," Xander inquired.

"It's not my place to say," the undead mage replied. "If you wish, ask Morana. She may or may not tell you."

"Are you sure that it's not all the undead crowded in here that makes you feel uneasy?" the Peacekeeper asked.

"No, they don't bother me. But this place," he looked up at Selandra with concern and confusion, "I can't put my finger on it, but it unsettles me and, at the same time, feels familiar. Strange."

"All will be revealed, Dampire," Tessa stated flatly.

Xander rolled his eyes, but kept his comments to himself. He wondered if it was her saying it or if the necromancer was speaking through Tessa. They came upon what looked like a stone slab lift. It had wooden rails on all sides with a small opening to enter.

Tessa stepped on the stone platform and said, "This will take us to Morana. Not directly though."

"Nothing is ever that simple, is it?" Xander replied as he stepped on the lift, holding the mage's hand.

"Nor is Morana," Tessa replied with a hollow chuckle. The stone platform vibrated and shook as it slowly made its ascent. There were no pulleys or chains lifting it up, it simply moved of its own accord by magical means. Selandra stepped over to the railing and got a panoramic view of the necromancer's domain. She was astonished by the sheer number of undead creatures. It was like looking down at a meadow that went on for miles, covered in reanimated corpses.

Xander teleported himself on the mage's back, sensing her anxiety and unease. "Now that's an impressive little army of dead things. Someone has been busy collecting recruits."

"If you think that is impressive," Tessa said impassively, "wait until you see the rest. This is what you would call the first wave. Morana has more of us than you can imagine possible."

Selandra looked at Xander, concern etched in her eyes as she silently gulped. The Dampire squeezed her shoulders as he whispered, "I know. I see them. At least we don't have to fight all of them at once."

"Oh, that's a comforting thought," Selandra sarcastically muttered, unable to wrap her mind around the size and magnitude of the necromancer's army of the dead. Scrapping of stone echoed above them as a granite panel moved away, creating a hole for the lift to enter. As the platform came to a halt, more of the undead greeted them, staring directly at the occupants of the lift with lifeless, cloudy eyes.

A grand courtyard greeted them, though everything appeared different than down below. There was no roof over the grand courtyard, the sky was stormy looking with purple and black clouds as tendrils of lightning streaked everywhere. The stone work on the walls was a mixture of granite, marble, and limestone and had black thorny vines growing on them. Blue glowing orbs were used in place of torches, giving off an eerie ambient lighting to the area.

What could be seen of the cloudless patches of the sky was strange. It had a hazy tint of brown and green. For a brief moment, Xander could have sworn that he saw people and tiny structures. Undead leapers clung on the walls like protective sentinels, ready and poised to pounce. Even in the open layout, the aroma of death and decay saturated the air as reanimated corpses stood quietly in varying degrees of decomposition. Droplets of rain fell from the eerie sky as Tessa stopped. She pointed to the entrance of a long winding ramp. "This is as far as I can go at this time. Morana awaits you at the summit of her tower. Stay on the ramp and you'll find her with ease, if you don't stray."

Selandra bowed her head. "Thanks, my old master."

Tessa chuckled as she placed a hand on the mage's shoulder. "I'm dead. That title and way of life are gone for me. You don't have to keep calling me that. I do hope that both of you will consider the offer Morana has for you." All merriment faded from her voice as she added solemnly, "I'd like to have you both on our side when Morana makes her presence known to everyone in all of Dragermora."

"If it means becoming the pawn of yet another conjurer, then I'll have to decline," Xander replied as he walked towards the tower.

The tower was obsidian black and had sigils and runes etched meticulously into the stone that glowed slightly. More vines snaked around it, but these were different from the other ones. The vines were a mixture of black, red, and green and had no thorns at all. There was no door, just an open entrance way. Several small windows lined the top of the tower, each had an orange glow coming from within.

Selandra walked in tandem with the Dampire up the ramp, the mage's footsteps echoing throughout the winding corridor. Each side had doors leading to other rooms and had the same eerie blue orbs lighting the way.

"How do you think our meeting will turn out," Selandra asked.

"Badly, with the way our luck has been recently. I'm not sure what to expect from her."

"Her dark sorcery is stronger than I anticipated," the mage stated as she moved closer to the wall on her left. She placed her hand on the cold, damp stone and shivered. "I can feel it. As if this place was actually alive. It doesn't make sense. How is it possible?"

"We can ask Morana when we go through there," Xander replied while pointing ahead to a sickly green door.

Chapter Twenty One

When they got several feet from the sickly green door and poised to knock, it opened on its own accord. Xander rolled his eyes. "Mages showing off once again."

"I'm far from being a mage," a sultry female voice answered from within. "Both of you may enter. We have much to discuss."

Xander walked in with Selandra following right behind him. The room itself was sparsely decorated with several small tables. The walls were lined with bookshelves, crammed with many different kinds of books. At the center of the room was a fire pit, the fire contained within it flickered and danced as though it was alive. Morana stood peering out one of the windows at the sky as rain came pouring down. She was wearing an elegant black dress that accentuated her curves. It was low cut, revealing her ample cleavage with an emerald pendant necklace nestled just above her breasts. Morana had a crimson sash around her narrow waist with a silver dagger tucked in it. Her alabaster skin appeared unmarred from the ravages of time, no signs of scars, and she was barefoot.

"Like this storm, I shall pour the contents of my realm into Dragermora and wipe out all that stands against me." The necromancer spoke as she brushed her long, silky brown hair away from her face. She turned around and looked at Selandra first, then she smiled brightly at the Dampire. "Have a seat. You two look like you could use a rest."

A cushy plush couch appeared in front of them. Selandra sat down as Xander stood in front of her protectively, crossing his little arms across his chest.

"Why do you want to do that," Selandra asked.

Morana walked towards them and let her gaze rake over their bodies. "Interesting bond you two share. Who exactly put those wardings on you, my child?"

"I may be small, but I'm *not* a child," Xander growled. "Why do you care about those?"

The necromancer bent down and put her hand on the side of the Dampire's face, causing her black eyes to glow. "Curious, indeed. How long have you had them?"

"Answer Selandra's question and I'll answer yours, Necromancer," Xander replied with a scowl.

Morana chuckled as she stood back up. "This world needs a thorough cleansing of both humans and supernatural beings. It's time for a new beginning and right a few wrongs. This *necromancer* title that you refer to me as is fitting and yet, misguided. I'm so much more than that."

"Cryptic. Imagine that?" Xander shook his head in disgust as he sat down next to his mage. "Why must you conjurers feel the need to be mysterious. It's annoying and serves no purpose, except to stroke your own ego. You're not what I expected to see. I imagined that you would have platinum blonde hair, clad in all black, wearing a cloak, and wielding a mystical black dagger crafted from bone."

"I shall tell all once you tell me how you came to have those wardings on your person."

"The Great Wizard Zerron placed them on Xander as a way to control him when I brought him to Le'orn not that long ago. He broke the Vampire Pact and is now in servitude to him."

"I see," Morana flatly stated. "Tell me, how did your bond form?"

"Zerron," Xander spat. "He forced this on us both so she could easily control me. He's a bastard and Sel here should have had a say in the matter. Meddling mages!"

"Is that how this little enchantress keeps you in line, my child? From what I can see, your feelings for each other goes both ways," Morana said as she walked around the fire pit, thinking to herself. "So, you're both unwilling victims to his machinations?"

"Zerron is my leader," Selandra answered with a slight shrug. "I don't agree with all his decisions, but I have to follow what orders he dispenses. I hate to see Xander like this but there's nothing that I can do." She hung her head and added with a sigh, "I have no power over Xander, of any kind."

Morana looked at the mage for a moment and then Xander asked, "Why did you want to have a discussion? I figured that you would rather us both be ripped to shreds by your reanimated playthings."

"I want to make you a proposal," Morana stated with a coy smile. "I can remove all the wardings on you, Xander. I have the knowledge and can easily break them for you."

The Dampire eyed the necromancer, annoyance visible on his visage. "What's the catch? Magic never comes cheap, so what's the price? Join you in your quest to destroy the world?"

"Not the world," Morana replied as a small cushion chair appeared beside her. She sat down with her fingers steepled under her chin. "I merely want to show my brothers that I can create life from death itself. For a long time, I've sat back in the shadows. Watching humanity toil and struggle to tame the land, yet they are like a disease. Destroying everything that they come in contact with like little toddlers breaking their playthings. The supernatural beings are only slightly better than the humans. You were a part of the last skirmish. You know what I mean."

Confused, Selandra replied, "What are you blathering on about? You're a supernatural being just like us. I feel like there has to be more to this. At least, some reason for all of your hate."

Xander reached over and grasped her hand. "I was a part of the Fae war, but I don't see how your plan for mass genocide fits in with it. Drop the cryptic routine and tell us why both sides vex you so much."

Morana sneered. "It's because of my brothers. They created them. Let them loose in the world without supervision. Each side killed my own creations just because they were different. Like they're so much better. Hypocrites!"

The Dampire and the mage looked at each other for a long moment before Xander said, "Your brothers? Are you referring to who I think you are?"

"Dracon and Gerbon," Morana hissed as she stood up, knocking her chair over. "Whom else would I be talking about? Being a vampire, you should know my story in all of this."

"Just because I'm part vampire doesn't mean that I was told bedtime stories or dark fables. If anything, I'm more of a cautionary tale not to go sticking one's prick where it shouldn't be or you'll get stuck with a *monster* like me."

Selandra smacked Xander on the back of his head. "Stop that! How many times do I have to say that you're not a monster before it sticks in that thick skull?" She looked at Morana and asked, "Are you claiming to be yet another one of them as well? A creator of Dragermora?"

"You say that like someone else has been claiming to be one." Morana narrowed her eyes at the mage suspiciously. "Whom do you speak of, young conjurer."

"We met, well I met Gerbon a few weeks ago. I still can't believe he had a hand in all of creation," Selandra stated, feeling bewildered and overwhelmed. "Don't tell me that you were there too."

"Gerbon. Dracon. Morana," the Dampire replied as he counted the names on his hand. He teleported all around the room frantically. Both Selandra and the necromancer could only watch as he disappeared and reappeared the best that they could, giving them a sense of vertigo.

He finally appeared next to his mage, holding a bit of parchment and a quill in his hands. The Dampire scribbled several lines and wrote several names down before asking with a cocked eyebrow as he snarked, "Who else is there that we should expect to come out of the woodworks next? Your mother? Grandmother? Second cousins? How many more of your relatives do we need to keep an eye out for?"

"Just us three, my child." Morana stood up and stepped up to the fire pit, the light from the flames flickered in her black eyes. "I know ignorance is the reason none know of Gerbon and myself, but that solely lies on Dracon's shoulders for his part in editing the history of the world. Do you want me to regale you with what occurred?"

"Why would it matter? What do you expect to come from it?" the Peacekeeper asked.

"War is coming to the world of Dragermora. This knowledge will help you decide which side you want to be on when the lines are drawn in the sands of time. I'm not going to force you to join me, everyone has a choice."

"Your *child* Merrick didn't give either of us much of a choice with his offer," Xander replied as his hand unconsciously rubbed his neck. Selandra reached out and grasped his other hand as he continued to speak. "Join you or die. That was the gist of his offer to Sel here. Me? Dying was the only option and I'm not ashamed to say that the prick nearly accomplished this."

Morana turned her head quickly, glaring at them with such anger that it caused Selandra to flinch. Her features softened as she asked, "So you're the Peacekeeper that Merrick has been obsessing over? My apologies for that. My magic has that side effect on those I reanimate."

Xander squeezed the mage's hand protectively. "When she refused his offer, Merrick attempted to end her life by stealing her life force."

"Did you slay him?" the necromancer asked as she tapped a finger on her chin.

"No. He's being held in Zerron's dungeon for his attack on me," Selandra answered.

"I'm half tempted to tear your throat out for that offense," the Dampire added, ready to pounce on the dark conjurer, but he had the strange urge not to act on it.

"My child, you couldn't hurt me even if you wanted to," Morana purred as she sauntered over to the Dampire.

She stroked his slick hair lovingly as he growled uncomfortably, "Why do you keep calling me a child? If you think our peace accord will stop me from killing you, you're dead wrong."

Selandra's anger was seething at the necromancer's intimate moment with Xander, her eyes pulsating as she balled up her fist to punch Morana. She glanced at the mage and chuckled. "My dear, it's not like the love you have for him. I see that you truly do love him and he you. Can't a mother love on her child that she hasn't physically seen in centuries?"

Both Xander and Selandra turned their heads, gaping at one another before looking back at the necromancer, blurting out in unison, "What!"

"That said, do you want to hear the truth? Xander is one of my best creations to date."

"I believe that you must have gotten senile in your old age. My mother was a succubus. I know that because she kept my father from killing me outright. What form of mind games are you trying to play here?"

Morana slowly backed away and returned to the fire pit. "None, but I shall divulge everything to you and let you make your own decisions. It's only fair, though it's difficult on me because I'm holding on to a glimmer of hope that you will join me."

"What about Selandra?" Xander piped up. "Is she included in your plan?"

"She is her own person and can choose her own path," Morana replied flatly.

"I'm right here, you know?" the mage snapped as she stood up. "Whatever he chooses, I'll go along with it. It's not like either of us have much of a choice anyway."

The necromancer walked over to Selandra and gripped her shoulder firmly, examining the mage intently. The Peacekeeper felt small and powerless under the woman's intense gaze, but she managed to stand her ground and not shy away. Morana spoke to Xander, but her eyes never strayed from the mage. "You say that this Zerron bound you two to each other and is the same person that warded you, my child?"

"Yes, on both accounts, but what does it matter?" Xander replied as he slipped off the couch. "Selandra is stuck with me and a pawn for the Great Wizard Zerron. I can't touch him or I would have killed him outright."

"I see. Did he also fashion that blade for you too?"

"I told you. He's a meddling old fool who uses us both as tools to do his bidding. Much like what you want for us, I'm sure."

Morana let go of Selandra and backed away. She extended her arm and Xander's weapon flew into her hand. The blade came to life, startled both Xander and the mage. The energy blade was as black as the necromancer's eyes. She twirled it around, testing it before extinguishing the blade and tossing it back to Xander.

"That's not possible," Selandra blurted out. "Only the rightful owner of the weapon can wield it. What just happened?"

"Sit down, get comfortable and I will tell all, now that I understand both of you and your plight with the Great Wizard Zerron," Morana answered with a knowing smirk.

Chapter Twenty Two

Xander put his weapon away as the Peacekeeper flopped down on the couch, feeling bewildered. He could feel her discomfort and distress so he curled up on her lap to help comfort his mage. Morana benevolently smiled, watching them hold each other. "You two look perfect for one another."

"Yeah, yeah. She's my *Bride* and we plan on having many fat little children. Zerron made us this way," Xander snarked. He knew that the mage wouldn't approve of his assessment, but it was a fact.

"Must you say it like that?" Selandra muttered as tears pooled in her eyes, threatening to spill out.

"It's true and you know it. I'm not going to lie and say that I have no feelings for you, Sel. In the back of my mind, I do wonder if we would be together if Zerron hadn't meddled with both of our hearts."

"For what it's worth," Selandra answered as she looked down at the Dampire, caressing his cheeks, "I'm grateful for his meddling. I never knew that I could love anyone like the way I feel for you, Xander Bane. I wish that you could accept this as a gift and move forward."

"I would, but I've been around long enough to know that what we have won't last." Selandra was about to protest, but Xander shushed her. "Don't. I've had so many lovers throughout the centuries that their faces have blurred over time. I fear the same fate awaits me once more and I don't want to face it. It's also partly why Vivian holds a large torch for me. She's seen me at my worst, when it comes to love, and it's why she threatened you earlier. I'm not worth the heartache that I will give you, Sel, but I can and will gladly give you the world, if it would make you happy."

As tears streamed down the mage's face, Morana commented, "That's what love is all about, my child. Risking one's heart for the sake of another, to be completely naked and under the scrutiny of another is difficult, but it's worth it. Every relationship has its purpose, both the good and the bad. That said, shall I tell all now or do you two lovers need some alone time?"

"Might as well," Xander replied as he wiped Selandra's cheeks dry. "Start with how I'm your son."

"In due time, my child. I'll get to it, but you need more of the story so that you can fully understand. I'll skip over Dracon's story that everyone has heard and if you say that you've talked to Gerbon, I can skip his as well. Where is he?"

"Imprisoned for creating supernatural beings without Dracon's stamp of approval. My domicile where I was residing before being forced into servitude is his prison. So, just tell us your story," Xander said as he sat up, nestling his small form comfortably against Selandra.

"Interesting. I never knew what happened to him. It's true that they created Dragermora. I have an advantage that neither could accomplish. Resurrection. They can create life and extinguish it, but neither can bring a life back. I did it just to annoy them in the beginning, claiming that I had to practice my skills because over time, there were plenty of dead things to choose from. Then, it happened."

"What?" Selandra asked.

"I got bold and tried my hand at creation. Among all my experimenting, I made the world's first vampire in the darkness of night. I wanted it to live like my brother's creations, but the only way it could survive was by drinking the blood from the living. When Dracon found out, he cursed them to burn in the warmth of the sunlight. I was furious. Why shouldn't my children have a chance to live like my brother's creations? If they had their way, my children would starve and feel the pain of hunger like no other entity on Dragermora. I fought back by having my children hunt their children. It was amusing seeing vampires making more vampires and a great way to mock my brothers at the same time. Some of my creations can procreate, but they tend to breed with other living beings. The exception being vampires. I sat back and observed, wondering why. Then, it occurred to me that all vampires were infertile and that Dracon and Gerbon cursed them to keep them from overpopulating. I wanted my vampires to have children of their own so I took control of a succubus and had her lay with your father. Vestal is cruel, even when having sex, but with my influence on them both, I was able to reanimate his dead seed and you were conceived, Xander."

"Father was thrilled to have me around," Xander sarcastically said. "Does he know about your little ruse?"

"He does now. I told him that I was the one responsible for your conception after I went to Crimson Pass. They were starving and I couldn't allow it to happen so I granted them blood slaves that would never die and could help them skirt that terrible punishment they unjustly received after the Fae war ended. My children were forced into that conflict because Gerbon's children wanted to control more of the world than Dracon's children. Vestal was upset, but when I told him what I told you, he softened ever so slightly. He calls you an abomination, but in reality, you are an evolutionary step forward, Xander Bane. The only vampire that doesn't need my assistance to procreate life."

Selandra held Xander tightly as a gasp of surprise escaped her lips. "Are you claiming that Xander is fertile? He can have children?"

"Yes. Which is also why Vivian wants him. I told her if there were to be a union between them, I'd have to revive her long dead womb for it to happen. You, Selandra, Xander can have children with you because you're alive and a magical being too."

"What does my magic have to do with it," the mage asked, feeling both curious and excited.

"Regular humans with no magic can't handle the birthing of a half breed. The magic forms a buffer because the child grows and feeds off the mother's magic so it doesn't kill her through starvation. For some reason, my goatmen found a way around this."

"I imagine being constantly raped by a different beast day and night, something is bound to happen," Xander coldly remarked.

"So, now that you know my story, what are your thoughts? Do you want to join your mother and put an end to my brother's hold on both of you or are you still looking to slay me?"

"You never said how you can wield Xander's weapon," Selandra answered, but then her eyes widened as the necromancer's words sank in. "Are you suggesting that Zerron is actually Dracon? Your brother?"

"If it's true, Sel," Xander replied, his thoughts churning with everything he knew about the Great Wizard, "it would explain how she turned on my blade."

"Magic doesn't lie. As a practitioner, you should know that *all* magic has the unique signature of the caster. Dracon's magic is all over Xander's wardings and on your bond. I know that he's been trying to find me. I've blocked his favorite tool from seeing my domain."

Selandra gasped, "You're the one blocking the Eye!"

"Yes, and I'm sure that it's upsetting him greatly. He won't see my attack on Dragermora until it's too late," Morana replied with delight as the sickly green door opened. Two undead ogres shuffled inside, haphazardly dragging the limp body of a man.

Xander cackled as they roughly tossed the man on the floor. "Look, Sel. Orimus has finally arrived to save the day!"

"You know this man," Morana asked as she walked over to Orimus.

"You see a man. All I see is a cowardly worm," Xander said as he hopped off the couch. The Dampire purposefully walked over and kicked Orimus in the head as he tried to rise up. "Garrett sends his regards, you sniveling buffoon."

Orimus groaned as he rolled over on his back, his eyes squeezed shut as he rubbed the side of the head. Xander reached down and pulled the assassin up and on to his knees. He opened his eyes and saw that he was face to face with the Dampire. Orimus growled as he spat, "Of course you would be here, *abomination!* Still looking to steal another bounty from me?"

"I'm here for my own reasons," Xander replied as he flashed his fangs. "Now, I can witness how the necromancer adds people to her undead army. Thanks for volunteering."

Orimus turned his head and looked around at his surroundings. Selandra walked over and was standing next to the Dampire. Then, his eyes fell on Morana and was immediately entranced by her beauty. The assassin stood up on wobbly legs and slowly shuffled his way over to the necromancer as she beckoned him.

"Come forward and join my army of the dead. I shall make you more powerful than you are now," Morana said in a seductive voice. Selandra could tell that the necromancer was using her magic to make him compliant. She put her hands on Orimus's shoulders to help steady him, his neck revealed two puncture marks and blood stained his tunic.

"I can give you everything that you desire. All you have to do is say 'yes' and all your dreams shall be realized."

Orimus sagged against her, his forehead rested against her shoulder. He caught a glimpse of the Dampire and the Peacekeeper and maliciously smiled. "I know that you are capable of doing what you claim," a blade slid out from under the sleeve, "with your death!"

The assassin repeatedly stabbed Morana in her stomach, causing a black ichor to spill on the floor at their feet. The necromancer grunted in pain each time the blade entered her body. Morana's eyes closed as more black ichor leaked from her mouth before she collapsed on the floor. Orimus leaned down and wiped his blade clean on the necromancer's clothes.

The assassin turned around, glaring at Xander with a smug grin. "And just like that, I'm rich beyond my imagination and I won't owe you anymore!"

"You still need to escape here in order to claim your prize," the Dampire pointed out. "If the bounty was an instant payment, my money pouch would have jingled."

Orimus walked over, gripping his knife tightly as he pointed it at the Dampire and the Peacekeeper. "By right, I claim the bounty! You'll not be stealing from me ever again, *abomination*!" As the assassin kept talking, Xander noticed that the necromancer was shifting around on the floor before she stood fully erect, her black eyes glowing with power.

"I'm not going to let either of you leave this place alive," Orimus threatened as he prepared to attack.

"I hate to break your heart, Orimus, but you didn't finish the job. Boy, does she look pissed at you," Xander replied as he pointed at the necromancer.

"You take me for a fool?"

"Always," Xander replied with a grin.

"He's right," Selandra blurted out. "She survived your assault. See for yourself."

The assassin finally turned as he drew near the mage and saw that the necromancer stood there, glaring back at him with her silver dagger in her hand. The blade pulsated as a black aura danced around it, as though it was alive.

All of her stab wounds rapidly healed before everyone's eyes as she coldly said, "For your attempt on my life, you've sealed your fate, assassin. Time to join my minions for all eternity!"

A blast of magical energy that resembled a dagger came racing towards the assassin. Wide eyed, Orimus yanked Selandra in front of him, holding on to her like a shield. The magic struck the mage in her stomach, causing her to cry out in pain.

"Selandra! No!" Xander roared as her body was dropped to the floor, hard.

The assassin cackled as he ran out the door, joyfully exclaiming, "I told you that I would cause you pain and suffering, *abomination!*"

Chapter Twenty Three

Xander rushed over and held the Peacekeeper in his arms, his lips quivering. The mage's body shook and convulsed as the necromancer's magic traveled throughout her body.

"Selandra," the Dampire anxiously cried out, desperate to see her open her eyes. "Fight it, Sel! I know that you are strong enough!"

Morana walked over as she slipped her silver dagger back in her crimson sash. She looked down at the mage and apologetically said, "I'm so sorry, Xander. She was never my intended target. She doesn't have long to live."

"*You* did this to her!" the Dampire hissed, his eyes turned black as his demonic side showed itself. "Take your bloody magic out of her and fix her! I know that you are capable of it!"

"Xander?" Selandra croaked out, sounding confused as blood sipped from her mouth, "Where's my... partner?"

"I'm here, Sel," Xander replied as he draped her in his lap, protectively holding her. "I'm not leaving you here all alone."

"Xander?" The mage's eyes finally found him. She reached up and caressed his face.

"Yes, Sel?"

"I...love..." the Peacekeeper rasped as her eyes went vacant, her arm fell limply to her side. Xander roared loudly and then he gasped. The Dampire clutched his chest, as if he had been stabbed. He had never experienced pain like this before. It felt like he was dying.

"Your bond with her has been severed," Morana said as she kneeled down next to the Dampire. "What you are experiencing is her death. It will pass with time."

Xander wailed as he lifted Selandra's dead body up and slowly walked over to the couch. He gently put her down as if she was as fragile as a porcelain doll. Xander rushed over to the nearest wall and repeatedly punched it, not caring if he broke his hands as he angrily screamed, "I told her this would happen! Any that I care about all die because of me! Why did it have to be her and not me, damnit! Selandra deserves to live a happy, peaceful life and all I granted her was pain, suffering, and death."

The Dampire felt a hand sternly grip his shoulder. He glared at the necromancer as she calmly spoke. "I can see that Selandra meant a lot to you, my child. Stop hurting yourself and let's talk about her."

"What's there to say? Orimus murdered my fucking mage!"

"Yes, he did. The man took your lover from you. I want to give her back to you."

Xander narrowed his tear shaped eyes at her. "For a price, I'm sure."

"Unfortunately, yes. It is required, if I'm to restore her."

"Maybe this is the best thing for her. She doesn't have to be with a *monster* anymore," Xander moaned as his little shoulders slumped in defeat. "Just take my life and give it to her."

"I can do that, but what you're feeling is the bond. You're experiencing her loss because that's what happens when it is broken. Dracon made it that way to keep you from killing her. I refuse to swap your life for hers, my child."

"What do you require," Xander asked, the muscles in his jaw twitching.

"The life of another. More specifically, the life I was cheated out of. The one responsible for your Bride's death."

The Dampire gutturally growled, "Orimus?" When the necromancer nodded, he added, "Consider him yours. Does he need to be able to move?"

"No, but he needs to be alive. Don't kill him, Xander. As much as I know that you want to, he needs to be alive to save her. I'm keeping her in place, which is causing Selandra a great deal of pain, so hurry. I'll have her prepared for the ritual."

Xander wiped his eyes as he closed them. He focused on Orimus, easily locating him through his blood signature. The Dampire sneered as he teleported away.

Orimus dodged the groping hands of the undead as he feverishly searched for the way out of the realm. The rain cascaded down in waves, like an invisible hand was grazing the strange clouds. The assassin yanked on the nearest door and rushed inside. The banging of fists on the other side of the door prompted him to use several bookshelves to barricade it. Orimus searched the room, hoping to find another exit, when he heard a familiar voice coming from the ceiling.

"It's bad form to cut and run from a fight twice in one day."

Orimus glared at the Dampire with his dagger in hand. "Aww. Did I hurt you with her death? I hope so! Come down here and let's finish this. I want to see the life leave your filthy eyes!"

Xander dropped down on the floor without making a sound with his arms across his chest. "You're still under the delusion that *you* can actually kill me? Care to do the dance of death?"

The assassin cried out as he swung and stabbed his dagger at Xander. The Dampire avoided each strike with ease, causing Orimus's rage to grow. Xander sneered as he snatched the assassin by his wrist. With a quick squeeze and twist, Xander broke it.

Orimus screamed as he dropped his dagger. He used his good hand and punched Xander in the face several times, which did more damage to the assassin than the Dampire. Xander kicked Orimus in each of his knees, buckling his legs as they bent inward, causing the assassin to crumble screaming to the cold stone floor.

"You asked if you hurt me," Xander sneered next to Orimus's ear. "Yes you did, my old friend. I'm going to show you exactly what it feels like to be me."

The Dampire grabbed the assassin by his arms. Combining the brute strength of both sides of his lineage, Xander methodically squeezed each of the bones until they shattered and splintered.

"No more..." Orimus gasped. "I beg you... just kill me..."

Xander didn't respond as he crushed the shoulder sockets and the collar bone. He yanked Orimus back, laying him somewhat flat on the floor. The Dampire broke more bones, working from the assassin's feet on up. Each break echoed throughout the room. Once Xander finished each leg, he stood on Orimus's hips. He stomped his feet several times, pulverizing the pelvic bone.

Orimus passed out from all the intense pain, which made the Dampire angrier. Xander teleported himself next to his head and slapped him around until he woke back up. As Orimus opened his mouth to plead, Xander broke his jaw at the mandible joints.

The assassin quivered and cried in agony as the Dampire went to work on his ribcage. They snapped like twigs with each blow from Xander's fists. Once he was finished, the Dampire sat down on Orimus and coldly said,

"Did I hurt you yet? What's the matter? Dampire got your tongue? Time for you to be useful to me."

He teleported them both back in Morana's chamber. Xander dragged the assassin over to the necromancer and left him at her feet. He sneered as he kicked Orimus in the side. "Consider your debt to me paid in full." Xander looked up at the necromancer and demanded, "Now, bring her back."

"Was it necessary to brutalize him?" Morana asked.

"I was holding back. He's alive and that's all that matters. Now you know that he can't escape or attack you again," Xander replied as he sat down on the couch. He put Selandra's head on his lap and stroked her cold cheeks. "Will she be one of your undead minions?"

Morana was quiet for a moment, which made the Dampire look at her. The necromancer pulled out her silver dagger and got down on her knees. She muttered an incantation, causing her black eyes to glow, as she slipped the dagger into Orimus's heart.

"A life for a life," Morana said as she extended her arm, pointing at the dead mage. A bright tendril of light beamed from the tips of her fingers and struck Selandra, causing her body to buck and shake. Morana locked her gaze on Xander and said, "In order for her to be revived, she'll need your blood."

"You want me to turn her into a vampire," the Dampire replied as he opened Selandra's mouth.

"No, this won't turn her but it will change her. She will be different, but that's to be expected when someone comes back from the dead. If you don't, she *will* be one of my undead minions, as you put it. There's no guarantee that she will still have feelings for you, my child, since the bond is gone."

"It doesn't matter," Xander said sadly as he used one of his claws to cut open his wrist. "Selandra can make the choice for herself this time. At least she will have a say in the matter."

His blood flowed into the mage's mouth as he pressed it against her lips. Xander wondered how much blood Selandra would require.

I'd gladly give her all my blood if it means that Selandra will survive this.

Morana walked over and placed her hand on the Peacekeeper's heart. She muttered an incantation that sent jolts of magic to the heart, forcing it to beat and pump the Dampire's blood throughout her body. Xander felt delighted as he heard Selandra's heart beating once again.

"No more blood is required, my child," Morana said. Several of the reanimated corpses ambled in the room and removed Orimus's lifeless body. The necromancer called her silver dagger back to her hand. "Let her rest. She needs it and we need to discuss another matter."

Xander nodded as he licked the cut on his wrist, helping it to seal faster and to stop the blood flow. He could see the color returning to the mage's skin, the wound from the magical attack was closing on its own. Selandra's breathing was even and unlabored. She whimpered softly as she rolled on her side, clutching her stomach. Xander lifted her head up and slipped out from under it. He gently set her head down on the couch and then he softly kissed the mage on her lips.

Xander walked up to the necromancer as she led him to a well concealed doorway on the back wall. They walked up a set of winding stairs that led to the roof of the tower. Morana waved her hand, causing a small hatch to freely swing open. The rainstorm continued to pour, but neither of them were concerned about getting wet.

"How badly do you want my brother's wardings off you," Morana asked as she looked off in the distance, her hands resting on the wet stone edge.

"Why would you want to help me? If your brother had the foresight to put them in place, doesn't that little fact tell you all that you need to know about me?"

"It does," the necromancer honestly replied. She looked down at the Dampire with a sad smile. "But I created you and I don't think it's right to hinder you with such crude and cruel magic."

"If you knew my history, you would do the same thing if you were in his place," Xander said, thinking about his life up to this moment. "I'm a beast that needs to be shackled. I'm a monster that can't be trusted."

"And yet, I stand up here with you. All alone with just a small dagger to defend myself."

"I never claimed you to be a bright girl. I could kill you easily enough, but you saved Selandra and our parley is still intact. Spit out what you want. I'm tired, wet, and in no mood for games."

The necromancer pulled out her silver dagger and created a small shield that kept the rain off of them. A small fire appeared beside them with purple/blue flames dancing around. She smiled as she said, "There. That should help dry you off "

The Dampire glared. "It would have been nice if you did this in the first place. Why bring us out here? Why not talk inside?"

"I didn't want to disturb your friend. I need this space if I'm going to break your wardings. The magic could hurt the mage and neither of us want that."

"What's the point? It's not like I can offer you anything in return, given your unique lineage."

"Oh, but you can," Morana replied as she walked around the Dampire, her hand grazing along his damp shoulders. "If you can give me the exact location of both of my brothers, I'll free you, Xander. My fight isn't with you and certainly not with your mage."

"But it will be if you go through with your plan," Xander countered. "We will be caught in the middle of this little war with your siblings. Fighting to survive."

Morana squatted down in front of the Dampire, looking directly in his eyes. "You misunderstand me. I want to break the wardings on you to show my gratitude for the information you have about them. That is my price."

"No, join me and my army? Doesn't sound like much of an offer for you."

"I've been around for a long time. The only constant in the world that has value is information. You have what I need and I'm prepared to give you whatever you desire for it. I can give you more, if my offer isn't good enough."

"Can you guarantee that none of your alliances will attack Selandra and myself? I don't mind the brutal carnage of war, but she shouldn't be a part of it."

"I can stipulate that you both are off limits, but we both know that won't happen. If an opportunity opens itself, people will take it during war. I can keep my undead off of you, but that's as far as it goes. Even if you both fought for me, my protection for you won't prevent people like your father from trying to assassinate you both."

Xander thought for a moment, weighing the pros and cons of the offer, "I'll always be hunted, no matter what. I'm a scourge in the eyes of the world. A trophy for someone's mantle. Selandra deserves a better life than what I can give her."

"Do you love her, my child?" the necromancer asked.

"Yes, which is why this is a difficult decision to make. With the bond gone, will she love me in return or was it all just a cruel joke crafted by Zerron?" Xander sighed as his little shoulders slumped. "Who in their right mind could ever love an abomination like me?"

"Love is more powerful and intoxicating than you realize. You recall what she said before she died in your arms?" As the Dampire slowly nodded, the necromancer wiggled her silver dagger in his face. The fire glinted off the blade as she spoke. "That's all the proof you need to snub out those doubts. If I break the wardings, I'll need to stab you with this. I don't like the idea of hurting you, but-"

"Blah, blah, blah," Xander retorted as he lifted up his tunic and vest, revealing his stomach. "I've already had a good pair of clothes ruined recently. Just do it and let's get it over with."

"Where is Gerbon?" Morana asked as she produced a small crystal ball. It hovered in the air revealing a map of the world. "Think of it and touch the ball."

Xander nodded as he pressed his finger on the crystal ball. In his mind's eye, the Dampire thought of the ancient stronghold and it appeared before them.

"Interesting," Morana commented. "I knew that there was something odd about that structure. I never would have guessed he lived there."

"He's imprisoned there and a part of the structure itself," Xander explained as he revealed more, showing where Gerbon was at. "Gerbon is literally the room itself. I'm not sure that I can point out the location of Le'orn. Zerron insisted that no one tell me or grant me a world map. You'd think that he didn't trust me."

The necromancer put a hand on his shoulder and said, "When I do this, I'll be able to track him down. Since you say Merrick is imprisoned there, I'll give him a little surprise that he won't see coming. I've blocked his gaze, but he's also hidden himself from my eyes. Once the wardings are shattered, he will feel it and might believe that you perished. I'm sure that he felt Selandra die. It's how he knows who to keep out of his domain, when he loses a mage, according to Tessa. I'm not going to lie, this *will* hurt."

"Pain and suffering is my middle name. Do it!"

Morana pushed the silver dagger into the Dampire's stomach, causing him to gasp and grunt. She twisted the blade while chanting a language that Xander didn't recognize. Morana smiled malevolently as Dracon's location revealed itself to her.

Chapter Twenty Four

Merrick dangled from the magical chains against the cold stone wall of his cell. His eyes were vacant as he stared at the floor. The mage was consumed with one thought.

Selandra.

How could she choose that thing over me? Doesn't she know that we're meant to be together forever?

At that moment, Merrick stood up straight as Morana's voice echoed in his head.

"Merrick, my child. It's time for the great cleansing to begin."

"I'm trapped, my dark one," the mage said aloud, shaking his shackles. "Zerron has cut me off from my magic."

Morana chuckled as she cooed, *"Allow me to change that, my child. Once I free you, you know what to do."*

Merrick's body trembled as he thrashed against the wall. The guards opened the door and stepped inside to see what was going on, their staffs were aimed at the prisoner.

"What do you think you'll accomplish, Merrick?" one guard asked.

"Yeah," the other one chimed in, "there's no escaping those bindings so knock it off."

Merrick's body stilled and sagged against the wall for a moment. The guards stepped in front of the prisoner, looking him over.

"You still alive, deserter?"

Merrick's head snapped up, his eyes glowing black as the shackles holding him glowed bright. His voice changed, having more of a feminine sound as he replied, "I've not been alive for a while. And now, neither will you two!"

The shackles exploded, sending piping hot shards of metal everywhere. The guards cried out as they got hit by the shrapnel. Merrick held out his hand, allowing his dagger to come to him. He gripped the handle tightly as he drew some of his blood on the blade.

The undead mage slashed his dagger, opening a rift. Alarms rang throughout the spire as Merrick summoned reanimated corpses to do his bidding. The guards attempted to flee, but Merrick closed the cell door. The guards fired wave after wave of magical attacks at the prisoner, but Merrick easily deflected them. The guards called for aid as several reanimated corpses stepped out of the rift, heading straight for them. Terrified, the guards fired at the corpses, but nothing seemed to affect them.

Merrick pointed his dagger at the guards and hit them repeatedly with his own magic, battering them just as his undead army reached them. The men cried out as the undead drew their own weapons and cut them down mercilessly. Merrick walked over to the cell door, opened it and said in his own voice, "Go and slaughter them all. Leave none alive."

****

Zerron paced back and forth in his study, concern etched across his wrinkled visage. He felt Selandra's passing and wondered if the Dampire finally killed her.

"I wouldn't be surprised if he did, treacherous creature," the Great Wizard muttered out loud to himself. "Oh well, I suppose that I should summon him and ask what occurred to her."

Zerron lifted his hand to activate the Dampire's wardings, but then he gasped like he got punched in the gut. The leader of the Peacekeepers dropped down on his knees, panting breathlessly. Once he regained his composure, Zerron effortlessly stood up. He leaned against his desk, wiping his brow. "And Xander Bane is no more. What a pity, but who could be responsible for this?"

The intruder alarm rang, causing the Great Wizard more concern. He marched over to the double doors and flung them open, grim determination set on his visage. Several mages ran up to him, panicking as they bowed.

"What is happening?" Zerron demanded.

"There's been a breach, Great Wizard Zerron," one mage replied.

"Then go outside and deal with the Interlopers," Zerron snarled.

"The breach is coming from the dungeon! It's been overrun with the dead!"

Zerron's face blanched as muttered, "How did Morana find her way in here?"

"What are your orders, Great Wizard Zerron?"

"Go seal off the dungeon, let none escape from-" The leader of the mages was cut off by screaming and swords clashing all around them. Zerron heard someone shout, "The dead are everywhere! How do we kill what's already dead?"

Zerron pointed at the line of mages fighting off Merrick's army. "You two! Go help them out!"

One mage hesitated. "What about you?"

"I said *go now!*" the Great Wizard growled, his eyes glowing brightly.

The two mages unsheathed their swords and charged after the nearest cluster of reanimated corpses. Zerron turned on his heels and went back into his study and slammed the double doors shut. He peeled off his robes and dropped down on the floor on all fours. Zerron's body painfully shifted and contorted, his wrinkled skin slipped off his body as scales and horns replaced his flesh.

Zerron stood up as the double doors were being banged on by the undead. He backed away in his dragon form and bellowed, "Morana! You dare defile my home with your filthy creatures! When I find you, your death won't be swift!"

The doors to his study flung open and Zerron unleashed his deadly fire on the reanimated corpses. The dead burned and crumbled to the floor as more marched towards the crimson dragon of the spire.

Discover what fate has in store for
Xander in

March of the Undead

The Xander Bane Chronicles: Book
Three

About the Author

Joshua Griffith is a Native American
Cherokee who loves to tell stories about the
paranormal and the supernatural, but adds a
twist of humor to alleviate some of the
inherent drama and suspense that can make
the characters seem more relatable. He grew
up in the eastern part of Oklahoma,
witnessing many strange and wondrous
things that went bump in the night. Joshua
Griffith currently resides in the Pacific
Northwest. As part of his path as an energy
healer, Joshua Griffith felt it would be good
idea to incorporate some of his experiences
in his novels. As they say, there's always a
hint of truth even in a good work of fiction
so it's up to you to decide which is truth and
which is hot air. Joshua Griffith invites you

to read his stories with an open mind because these tales are works of fiction, but ask yourself this: Could this really happen?

If you enjoyed A Storm on the Horizon, please do leave a review. I love reading them because they encourage me to get better and keep the stories coming!
If you want to check out my other work, scan the QR code below.

www.ingramcontent.com/pod-product-compliance
Lightning Source LLC
Chambersburg PA
CBHW070545260626
47161CB00002B/509